Waiting for Otto

Ron Rude

PublishAmerica
Baltimore

First printing

ISBN: 1-4137-5347-7
PUBLISHED BY PUBLISHAMERICA, LLLP
www.publishamerica.com
Baltimore

Printed in the United States of America

For Karen,
who hung the photo, gave me the transcript,
breached some family silences,
and who carries out so well a long tradition of loving and serving.

Acknowledgments

Thanks go to Mr. Duane V. Retzloff, who gave permission to borrow from his book *The Retzlaff-Brandenburger Family History Book*, 2002. None of the story herein borrows directly from that book, but keeping track of families and generations, real or imagined, is much easier when such a comprehensive work is available as a roadmap.

The only material borrowed directly in *Waiting for Otto* is that from the Bible and from the Lutheran Churches' authorized version of the *Service Book and Hymnal,* 1958, and used by permission of Augsburg Fortress.

Resources consulted other than these mentioned, and other than family artifacts, include:

The Germans from Russia: Children of the Steppe, Children of the Prairie (videotape), Prairie Public Broadcasting, Inc., 1999.
Of German Ways, LaVern Ripley, Dillon Press 1970.

Thanks also go to all the "old folks," those a generation or two ahead of me, who have told me their own stories ever since I was a child. It seems to me that those stories, whether simple or complex, funny or sad, painful or proud, are critical to each new generation's own self-image and self-perception. Just as importantly, such stories remind younger people that that dotty octogenarian in the rocking chair may be someone to emulate rather than someone to take for granted.

Chapter One

Reunion: Bigfork, Montana: 1982

"The road is good," Charles said. "Narrow and dusty, but maintained enough for a pickup or even a sedan. Of course…" (Charles always did like to needle people) "…it's pretty steep over the side, so maybe flatlanders shouldn't go."

That was a challenge, so there were three carloads making the climb of 5,000 feet in 15 miles. Drivers kept the vehicles separated so nobody had to eat too much dust. Loose stones popped under the tires on the outside turns where flatlanders indeed did not want to look over the edge. At turnouts passengers from three generations snapped pictures of the blue-black mountains undulating away to the horizons.

Dizzy, who had grown up in Illinois and married into the family, lived up to her nickname and became the butt of teasing, not only from Charles but from any others who decided they didn't mind the steepness. She was the only one who let out little shrieks on those outside corners, who clung white-knuckled to the dash as if already braced for the crash far below, who stayed in the car rather than climb the stairs of the tower, who shut her eyes almost all the way home and collapsed with a headache for the rest of the day.

Selma, age 93, had a wonderful day. She had never been so high up, never seen mountains from the perspective of a mountaintop, never felt the little stomach-thrill, which certainly does come from looking over the edge.

"I don't mind that it is steep," she said, grinning at Charles. "I'm ninety-three years old. I have nothing to lose."

For the rest of the reunion she was the hero for that remark. "Granma Wollerman ain't afraid of nothin'," they said. "Ninety-three and still up for some fun. Ain't she somethin'?"

Of course Selma had to be helped in and out of the car, and she couldn't climb the steps of the tower at all. Her knees simply didn't bend well enough.

But she shuffled around near the car, looking first west where somewhere far off was Washington. Daughter Katherine lived there. And south somewhere across more mountains was Wyoming where lived John, here for the reunion, and farther south yet in California was the home of Conrad, retired and here for the reunion, too—the one who took Selma to the beach and Knott's Berry Farm, both of the boys comfortable because they knew how to stretch a working man's paycheck.

Far, far away west, in a distance so great Selma thought it might be like the distances between Russia and North Dakota, was Manila, where Selma had never been because, as she joked, "I can't find a Greyhound that goes over there," and where was memorialized Fritz, beautiful Fritz, killed by the Japs attacking his ship when the war was almost over, that death laying upon Selma another burden at a time when Otto's troubles were still fresh wounds, and she had already been hurt far more than she thought she could bear.

So long ago, and so much pain, and yet the Lord had seen fit to let her live to 93 and see all her living children and some of their children and some of theirs, too, and most had been able to live happy enough. Sure, troubles they had of their own, but none now suffered starvation or fear or the wrenching loneliness or the exhaustion of years and years of work and work with no hope in sight.

That was good. Good for them. And good that she, Selma, had lived beyond it to a peaceful old age, alone of course, but able to travel yet, able to cook for herself and do some crocheting and read the Bible a little every day.

She looked to the east, too, where more mountains stretched away, and far on the other side would be the prairies rolling and rolling with grass and wheat and the wind and the sky of no ending. That was where she had her elder's apartment in LaMoure, with good heat and hot water and a bathroom. If she did not feel like cooking, meals were ready-made at the Senior Center, and there were some people to play cards with, although some of them were not so fun because they could no longer remember the rules, or even hold the cards sometimes.

And if she had worries there she could call on Lorraine who was just fine to help if things weren't too busy on the farm, or on Elizabeth who was only a few blocks away and had a nice house and husband with an office job.

The reunion had brought them all to Charles and Janey's house at Bigfork, all Selma's living children, even Daniel who maybe could have made things better if he had helped out, but now it was too late to worry about that anymore, and Daniel was an old man himself.

In the evening Janey and the other girls began setting out the food. There were long tables of fruit salads, string beans in bacon-flavored mushroom sauce, scalloped corn, barbecued ribs, mashed potatoes, pies and cookies and ice cream—good American farm food. But also pickled beets and dill pickles and a huge bowl of borscht and loaves of fresh dark bread—good Russian-German foods.

Selma thought how she had taught them to do that, so is plenty for everyone, and all on time and all tasty like a meal should be. She saw that the granddaughters did much of the cooking, much of the setting-out, so they must know, too. That was how it should be, a good meal was a blessing, and when there was food it was always worth the work, and the young should learn from the older ones.

A good thing those granddaughters had learned, but Selma wondered if they could do it when in the house was only a bit of milk and stale bread and a stick of sausage left from last fall's butchering, with the chickens starving so there weren't enough eggs, and the cow drying up and no money to pay a grocer.

So much they didn't know, too, these granddaughters. What could they know of $35 a month, and that from the county so it was shameful. Her children knew how it was with no money, especially the older ones, but the granddaughters didn't know. Better they didn't. *Better is forgotten,* Selma thought.

Still, there was Otto. They did not know of Otto either, except that he had left and made life hard for Selma and her children.

And they did not know that, about Otto, Selma had something on her mind, something that needed to be done before it was too late.

Many times Selma had asked Janey and the other girls, "Have you told your children about your father?" always meaning about his leaving, though not saying it.

"No," they would say. "We don't talk about that."

"About Wilbur?"

"Nothing, Ma."

"Good," Selma would say. "We should not talk about that."

So the grandchildren did not know what Wilbur had done, did not know about Otto being a good man. They would not know about Ludwig, Selma's older brother, and Henry, the younger brother, who had been her strength at times more than Otto her husband. And yet her brothers were forgotten by the family, only Otto was remembered at all, and that in shame.

She watched the granddaughters clear away the meal, scrub the tables, do the dishes, their movements quick and practiced, a place for everything, everything spotless. Some of the men brought out some beer and a bottle of whiskey, and the visiting gradually separated into two groups, one around the booze, one around the coffee pot.

Ach, Selma thought. *And that never goes away. Those bottles belong to the devil.* She had told them and told them and told them, but some didn't listen.

But, after a time, she had decided maybe it was better not to talk about that either. It had led Otto to…

She could not think it. These younger ones…if only they knew what it could do.

There must have been close to a hundred people. It was confusing to count them and Selma only made it just past forty each time she tried. They moved around too much…some in the house, some out on the lawns, some in the garage where more tables and chairs were set up.

Summer night came on, cooling fast outside but still warm in the house, and no mosquitoes even though people were in and out all the time. She could hear murmurs of conversation rising and falling, sometimes a burst of laughter in the darkness outside, nothing loud enough to be a nuisance. Even the drinkers kept the noise down, though a couple of them did some quarreling before they quit. It became late, much past Selma's bedtime, and Janey and the other girls kept asking, "Don't you want to get to bed, Ma?"

She did. She was tired from the day. But the evening was so nice she didn't want to get out of the soft chair, and the time was coming.

"Look at what I started," she told them, looking around at all the people, some of whom she didn't really know.

How had she done that? How had she done all of it? Ninety-three years old, still getting shorter and wider, her hair so thinned it was hard for the girls to fix, the skin on her arms hanging as if it did not want to stay on her bones anymore, yet her internal parts working as they always had. She could eat a good meal, walk without help, feel her heart pumping just like it did when she was a girl, when they had all fled the Russians, when Otto had come to her—when she had thought each day she could not make another step, could not live another burden however slight and yet more had come, and not so slight either.

"All this came from me," she said again, looking out the window toward the garage lights.

After a time she whispered to Janey, "Have you told your girls about your father?"

"No, Ma. I've told you fifty times. We don't talk about him."

Ninety-three years old, and her own daughters were grandmothers, some many years already, and no one, no one but Selma Wollerman could speak for Otto ever again. When she said that to herself she shivered, and ever so slowly she pulled on her red sweater. She had always thought it was best not to talk about it, but now these last few years, she had begun to think maybe a man should be remembered for more than his mistake. Even her own children tried not to think of their father...

"Janey, Janey," she said urgently.

"What is it, Ma? Are you feeling sick?"

"Get the photographs and letters."

Janey would know which ones. And Janey was a good housekeeper, too. She would know right where they were.

"It's late, Ma. I don't want to go rummaging around for them right now."

"Ya. It's late." Selma was tired. *But in the morning*, she thought. *In the morning.*

"Tomorrow then," she said. "In the morning you find them."

"Sure, Ma. But we've all looked at them. Why do you want them?"

"I think I'll go to bed now," said Selma. She pushed herself to her feet and moved stiffly to her room. She had been sitting too long.

She was awake by six. Janey was still asleep, so Selma puttered about the kitchen making coffee and a slice of toast from the white bread which Janey used, good enough for a sandwich but too fluffy for good toast, which should be firm and not so dry. She was anxious to see the photos again.

They were so few.

One was of a dark-haired, smooth-skinned young woman, just her shoulders and head, the picture taken from above and behind the shoulder so you could see she was holding the child, Otto, while he slept. The mother was beautiful and she looked so tenderly at the round, sleeping boy. Selma thought their lives could never have trouble.

Another was of a dozen immigrants in their bulky clothes posed on board the ship, *President Lincoln*, before they entered New York harbor, Otto standing among them, looking solemn but very sure of himself.

Still another was a large photo, touched with muted colors, proud Otto in tight uniform astride a sleek military horse on parade somewhere in Germany. Three years he had been a soldier there for the Kaiser; three years on those powerful horses, everything polished, the brass and the saddles and his knee-high boots.

A few more were of farm houses on the prairie, children lined up in front, and a blurred picture of Otto plowing with four horses. One was of Selma posed alone for the photographer, another of her with Wilbur and two of the children.

And a few letters, Otto's letters to her.

That was all.

So little left. At one time, remembering the despair, she had thought even these should be thrown away, but instead she had given them to Janey.

And now she had decided it was not good that they did not talk about it. Ninety-three years old and she could remember it all but no one else could and it was time.

"Grandma. You're up already," Charles said to her.

"Yah. Is Janey coming now?"

"In a minute. She's brushing her teeth."

"Yah," Selma chuckled. "She doesn't yet have to take them out to do it." She wished Janey would hurry up, and as soon as Janey came into the kitchen, Selma asked again for the photos.

"Let me get my coffee first," Janey said. "What's the hurry?"

At first Selma didn't answer, so much going through her head that she felt she might get confused.

"We must talk about it now," Selma said finally. "We must talk for all who will listen. They should know about your father. They are here and if they will listen they must hear it all."

Janey set down her cup. She had not done her hair yet and it stuck out in gray bunches from her head like a crazy woman.

"You always said to leave it behind. We have a good life now. Why bring all that up?"

"They should know about your father," Selma said.

"Why, Ma?"

"Janey, get the photos and tell them they must listen. I am ninety-three years old."

Sighing, scratching her hair, Janey left the kitchen.

And Selma Retzlaff Wollerman, ninety-three years old, feeling her

13

heart pumping strong but just a little faster than usual, began thinking what she would tell first, and what after that.

She hoped they would listen.

Chapter Two

1900

Soon she would have to clear the table, but if she did not move maybe Vater would keep talking and reading the Bible. She was so full she was getting sleepy.

It was dark outside and the kitchen was usually lit with one kerosene lamp, but tonight, for company, Mutter had lit two more. One sat on the shelf of the cookstove, one on the table, one on a shelf high up the door to the front room. From November until almost April the house would be dark so often, and the kerosene stink would always be with them. But with so much light tonight it was easy to see the calendar with the days of November under a drawing of a new plow and the words: *John Deere Implement.*

"Selma is the cook now." Mutter had laughed when they set the table, because it was the first time Selma had made strudel by herself. She had stretched the dough a bit at a time, first making a flat, round sheet of it with the rolling pin, then, with her fingers, rolling the edges thinner and thinner. She did not yet know how to pat it across her arm like Mutter did, so she had been clumsy and torn the thinning sheet of dough more than once, but at the end she had seven or eight nice small rolls, which she chopped into pieces to cook with the potatoes.

So they had strudels eaten with lots of butter, and potatoes and some fried pork sausage and fresh milk and some *schwarzbrot*—dark bread, and Mutter had brought out from hiding some brown sugar for the children to sprinkle on one more slice of the schwarzbrot for dessert.

Sometimes when Vater did not like what had been cooked he talked about plagues on the land. But when they had strudels and the neighbors were there to visit he would say, "The land of milk and honey after all." The children knew he would soon talk of another place when he said it.

"Remember this day in which you went out from Egypt," Vater read tonight, *"from the house of slavery, for by a powerful hand the Lord brought you out from this place."*

He was always in German reading, which was comforting for Selma to hear because it was the language she knew, but sometimes it was confusing, too, the Bible with its big words, and in *schule* Selma was learning English. Some of the words were the same and some were not, so she could understand some of both, read in English and in German. The English was easier to read, the German easier to speak and understand. Sometimes she just got it all mixed up.

"And it shall be when the Lord brings you to the land of the Canaanite," Vater read on, *"the Hittite, the Amorite, the Hivite, and the Jebusite, which He swore to your fathers to give you, a land flowing with milk and honey."*

"When I first come over I looked up and down the James River, but the Swedes and Norwegians got the bottom lands and they don't sell. And they are getting filthy rich," Johann Flagen said, "so they think the Book of Exodus is about them."

Vater laughed, then shook his head. "They are the Hittites and Amorites," he said. "In Russia we had so much, and here…here I think it takes twice the work for half the crops."

"Yah," Johann Flagen said again. "I got only one field is flat and easy, and the oats went thirty bushels. Over at LaMoure I talked to a Norwegian. He got a field same size, it went fifty bushels. And he don't have to haul it so far to town."

"And the river they have, with fishing, and ice easy to get for the ice

houses. Maybe the Bible says we have to go conquer the Norwegians."
Vater laughed. "It says God swore to give us that land."

Flagen laughed with him.

That was the kind of thing that confused Selma. She knew what it
was to swear, because the teacher slapped the boys with a ruler if they
did it, and told them there would be no swearing in this *schule*...school.
But now the Bible said God swore.

"*Unser leighte*, our people, I think are smarter than a bunch of
Norwegians," Vater said seriously. "We make something of this poor
land, and then we buy them out."

"Yah." Flagen laughed some more. "Conquer them, and no bullets
flying."

"Ah, but what we had in Russia," Vater said. "*Verdammen Rusiche*,
promises in one hand and stealing with the other."

Muter scowled at Vater when he swore like that, though it didn't
seem to stop him. Selma thought that whenever he talked about Russia
it was the same. Things had been so much better there, but the Russians
had taken it all away, stolen it, and then had begun the long journey to
North Dakota, and he always was swearing with it.

Selma had only been two years old. She did not remember any of it
except something frightening about the sound of a boat, and something
about Emilia...Emily...puking. Emily remembered it much more, and
so did their brother Ludwig, who had been eleven. Emily had been nine
years old and now was eighteen, all grown up, a woman like Mutter.

Sometimes Selma asked Emily, "What was it like to live in Russia?"
It seemed that it must have been a good place because Vater said so, but
Selma couldn't picture it.

"We had a good house, warm in winter, cool in summer, not like our
house now," Emily had answered one time. "But Vater was always
about the Russians complaining the same. And I was frightened of
them, though they did not come to our village very often."

So Selma was a little afraid of Russians, though she had never seen
one. Mutter did not complain of them. She only talked about the
village, the village. Selma could not understand that, because she knew
about towns like Kulm, but how could anyone go to their fields if they

lived in town? Mutter said the village in Russia was better because all the people were close, all the houses were close. North Dakota was too much distance from others, too lonely, all the houses way out in the fields of the scattered homesteads.

But that part about the house sounded good to Selma, because in winter no matter how much coal was burned in the kitchen and the front room stoves, the upstairs bedrooms were so cold sometimes the chamber pots had ice on them. Even when they hung old blankets over the windows the wind would come in a little and fine snow piled up on the sills. Selma would huddle under enough blankets to crush her, and when little Martha had lived the two of them would huddle together, and even now sometimes Selma would climb in bed with Emily but still they were cold. In the morning when she had to use the pot she waited until she was ready to burst because she didn't want her bottom to touch the freezing rim.

In the summer it was the other way, some nights so hot in the bedrooms nobody could sleep until early morning when the prairie breeze began again and blew through the open windows. The curtains blowing in the faint light were pleasant to remember because it meant the house was getting comfortable, but still there was not much more sleep because by that time Vater was already going to the barn, and he would let the screen door slam when he went.

And even these things were better than the sod house she remembered from the first couple of years. Bugs everywhere, and garter snakes, and it was always dark, and once a horse grazed on top and fell through, a big hoof thrashing around by Emily's head.

A warm house in winter, that she would understand. But the Russians she could not. She thought that in North Dakota there were no Russians, though the teacher sometimes called her "Little Russky."

"*Nicht Rusiche*," younger brother Henry had shouted at the teacher when she tried it on him his first day in school. "Not Russian. *Nur Deutsche*. Only German."

The teacher had been angry at his shouting, but she quit calling him a Russky.

Selma's older brother Ludwig had not been in school for a long time. He was working the farm with Vater and more land to get started on his own. At home still with Selma were just Henry and Emily, though Emily had a man visiting her.

"You will marry this Martin Seibern?" Mutter had asked Emily one day when the two women did not know Selma was listening.

"Yes, when he is ready," Emily had answered.

Then Selma had to ask Mutter, "What is it to marry?"

Mutter had laughed. "It is as with Vater and me," she said. "We are man and wife."

Selma thought it must be something good, because Mutter and Vater talked to each other like friends, only they didn't have to go to school to see each other. They were always home, and even when Vater was out in the fields sometimes Mutter would come along when Selma and Henry brought out the lunches, and Mutter and Vater would talk and talk to each other while they ate.

In the country school Selma had some other girls she talked to, but she did not have a friend like some of the others did. She had tried, but the girls turned her away. She did not know why, but she thought maybe it was something about the teacher calling her a Russky.

"When can I get married?" Selma had asked.

Mutter had laughed some more. "For that you must wait," she had answered.

It seemed like everything Selma asked Mutter about, that was the answer. Some days she thought all she was doing was waiting, and for what she didn't know.

Vater and Flagen looked alike, both with black beards that wiggled when they chewed and when they talked, both men nodding while the other spoke.

"*Unser leighte*, our people, they were real pioneers in Russia," Vater said to Johann Flagen, who nodded and nodded.

Now Selma listened carefully, still feeling her stomach stretched around the strudels. "Pioneer" was a word they read in English in a book at *schule*, and it was the same in German. She knew something about the pioneers who had gone on long journeys in covered wagons when there were no roads. Mutter said her cooking cabinet was something that pioneers had brought to North Dakota. It had wooden doors on the bottom, a square board that pulled out for preparing food, and glass doors on the top where dishes and spices were stored. When Mutter was cooking big meals she always said the cabinet was not big enough, and maybe the pioneers should have kept right on going west with it.

Outside at recess all the children laughed at the picture of a covered wagon the teacher had drawn on the blackboard. "It looks like my grandma's bonnet stuck on a grain wagon," one of the boys had said.

So even though Selma did not have a picture in her head of Germany or Russia, only of North Dakota, she did have a picture of covered wagons when Vater talked about the journey his great-grandfather had taken from Germany to Russia.

A grandma's bonnet pulled by horses. It made her smile to think of it.

"My great-grandfather to Russia went," Flagen said between bites of strudel. "But that is all. The rest, we are *Bayerischer*, Bavarian. There we stay. And the mountains I miss. But not the Kaiser's army. I am a farmer, not a soldier. So, North Dakota."

"A civilization they built with their bare hands in Bessarabia," Vater said. When he got started on it he had to say the whole thing, no matter what others wanted to talk about. "From nothing. Those Turkish pagans for a thousand years had it and made nothing. The Russians could make nothing of it. They had to bring in Germans, and *unser leighte* made it a land of milk and honey."

Unser leighte. Words that Vater said often. Selma thought of it when the teacher called her a Russky. It might be there was *unser leighte*, and there was everybody else. When Vater said it he sounded as if it was something to be proud of, but when the teacher called her "Russky," it didn't sound that way. So, another thing she didn't understand with the two languages.

"Here the leftovers we get," Vater went on. "We leave our land of milk and honey because it is being stolen from us, and then we get here for the leftovers."

"Yah, no feasting on this kind of land," Johann Flagen said, his beard touching his chest each time he nodded. Then he looked up from his plate as if he had just thought of something. "But the meal is good, Maria," he said. "The meal *ist sehr gut*."

"Karl, it is better to have this land than nothing," Mutter said finally. "You complain too much."

They were quiet for a moment. Then Vater laughed. "I am missing the homeland," he said. "Today the weather and the crops I already complained about. So what is left for tonight is homeland."

When he says that, soon he will sing the homeland song, Selma thought, *and my ears will hurt. Mutter will shake her head, but he will sing, and he will get tears in his eyes.*

And in great, rough noises he did sing:
"God bless you, my homeland...my cradle...I am yours till death
The fruitfulness of the Black Sea...keep us German and pure
Until we rest with our fathers
Im heimatlichen Schoss!...In the cradle of our homeland."

Selma and Henry covered their ears with hands, and Vater laughed at them.

"Yah, it is hard, even when there is plenty of land," Johann Flagan said, and now it was Vater's turn to be nodding. "But in Russia I think there is war coming, and if the Czar is weak, nobody will be safe. And in Germany the Kaiser, the Prussians, everything is for the army."

"But these Americans like war, too," Vater said. "This Cuba. And now China, this Boxer Rebellion? What are these for Americans?"

Selma couldn't understand anything when they talked about war. People shooting each other, but that was too terrible to think about it. Mutter thought so, too, because when Selma had asked, Mutter had answered, "We don't talk about that."

She thought again about if she was a Russian. Mutter and Vater had argued one day about Vater's coat. "It is old," Mutter had said, pointing to the frayed cuffs. "You have for twenty years worn it. And it looks just like Russia."

The children at school had laughed at it, too, more than once, when Vater drove up with the horse and sleigh in winter. He would jump out and say, "Come, Selma, come, Henry," and smile and bow to them, making fun, the fur coat belted tight high up on his waist, and wide below, like a dress almost to his ankles.

"*Ach*," he had told Mutter about the coat. "It is warm still. And here…" he pointed at a picture in the Sears Roebuck catalog, "…what does this say? *Russian*. I can that much English read. *Und $28.00*. I can that read, too. The most dollars on this page. So it is the best coat."

Selma had looked at the picture. Vater had been right. "Russian buffalo calfskin coat, the best fur coat ever made for $28.00," she read aloud.

Vater laughed and laughed, slapping his knee. "Maria, Maria. Did you hear that? The best fur coat ever made."

Mutter had just smiled and shook her head.

"And you, Selma, you have saved me from a new coat to buy," Vater had said, and took her in his lap.

Mutter had shook her finger at Selma, but all of them were laughing, and it had been a time when Selma didn't care about wars or Russians or even friends, a time when she thought North Dakota must be a good place even if Vater said Russia was better.

Vater and Johann Flagan got up from the table and went to the front room. Selma knew what that meant. It was time to clear the table and wash the dishes.

"Henry can do the dishes tonight," Mutter said. "Selma was the cook."

Henry stamped his foot, but Mutter slapped him on the bottom. That was that. Henry should know better. Dishes always had to be done. Three times a day the same thing.

Selma was ten years old, and she understood it did no good to be angry about the dishes. It was the same with carrying out the chamber pots, sweeping the floors, carrying in coal for the stoves, pumping water, filling the kerosene lamps, feeding the chickens their grain, picking eggs, bringing in the cows from pasture, churning butter…so many things Selma was helping with every day, and now the cooking, too, and learning to milk the cows.

She did not understand about Russians, but she did understand about the work.

1904

Almost the last day of threshing the oats, and Vater was complaining the crops were poor. After the crews and the women ate supper and the dishes were done Selma had milked two cows while Henry did the other two. She didn't mind milking as long as Henry got the ones that kicked. He was still one to drag his feet getting the work started, so Selma had been first, taking the two gentle ones, and ignoring Henry when he complained.

The cows were still hot from the September day, and Selma didn't want their stink on her, so she pushed her scarf down on her forehead before she leaned against the cow's flank. Pulling and pulling, she brought the streams of fresh milk into the pail, stopping only to squirt out to the cats who waited for a taste. Sometimes she was surprised at how strong her hands had become. When she had first tried the milking when she was ten or eleven she could barely finish two teats before her hands cramped up. Now she could do all four cows in less than ten minutes each, without stopping.

The crews were made up of any available men and boys, and sometimes women, too, anyone strong enough to pitch grain bundles all day and handle the teams of big horses, two on a wagon. Ludwig was home to help but would be gone when the machine would go on to his land, as it would to the other farmers. Everything was a hurry, hurry, while the weather was good and the grain still dry.

The women also took care of the house and the barnyard and had a long day of cooking. In the evening it was the men who put up the tired horses, shut down the steam engine, and greased the machinery so it was ready for the next day.

The roaring and popping of the machines were louder than anything else on the prairie except a wind storm, and it hurt their ears, and they were all glad when it was quiet again. The noise had been worse when the machine was in the barnyard, but the last stack was being made out in the ravine.

No one had been stuck with a pitchfork on the Retzlaff place this season, no teams had run away and hit the long flying belt, no rocks had gone through a binder causing a breakdown, which would send Vater to Kulm or Edgeley or far away to Jamestown looking for repair parts.

"I am tired, Maria," he had told Mutter at supper. "But we finish this harvest with all our fingers."

"And still you complain." She had smiled back at him.

Selma thought that Mutter was like the threshing machine. Nothing could stop her. No matter how fast the crews threw in the grain bundles, the machine chopped them up, blowing the high stream of golden straw out the long tube into the growing pile behind, steadily dribbling the precious grain through the short tube into the sacks alongside.

Working, working, working, the crews got tired every day and had to quit before dark, but the machine was still going as it had in the morning. And Mutter was like that machine even at night, still going on, finishing one day and getting ready for the next.

Now Selma was fifteen, and she was proud she could do everything Mutter could do in the kitchen and the farmyard, except some of Mutter's special recipes from the old country did not come out the same. "Selma cooks this," Vater would guess, or "Mutter cooks this." It was a game, and more and more he would lose the game because he could not tell the difference.

She was just over five feet tall and she had not grown taller for a couple of years, but she was still hoping she would. She liked to look at herself in the mirror, though Mutter would scold her if she spent too much time in front of it. She had black hair, big, dark eyes, a pointed nose in a round face, smooth skin, and nice, even teeth, which she didn't have to hide when she smiled. In the summer she had a new dress from the catalog, delivered to Kulm. She had waited and waited for it to come, and when it did she had stood many times smoothing it over her tiny waist. She thought a boy would like to look at her because she was not skinny, not fat, rounded but strong, too.

Of course a boy would not like to look at her now, squatting under the cows, her hair greasy from days of sweating, her old dress made from flour sacks dirty and smelling, too. She would like a bath, a real bath, soaking for a long time, but in the harvest, with all the cooking, there was not time enough to heat water for real baths, and the summer kitchen barely cooled by morning enough to work in there. Heating more water would make it worse, and it would be midnight before it was done, and then to get up at five o'clock again the next day.

It was just a sponge bath when she could, but everyone else was the same. *Everybody is working hard and smelling bad,* she thought and laughed to herself. Everybody knew it, and nobody said anything about it.

But even if she had been clean and wearing her new dress, there was no boy whom she knew to look at her. There were boys on other farms, and some of them she had gone to school with, and sometimes she saw them at the church on Sunday, but they were like the men, working all the time or gone off on their own or even going to the new *hauptschule*, high school, in Kulm. Selma knew she was not going there. She had not been in school now for many years, so she knew her English was getting no better, but she remembered what she remembered, and she spoke a bit of English with Ludwig and Emily and with some of the work crews, and she read the Sears/Roebuck catalog and a few books in the house, but the most was German.

Some days she wondered if any boy would look at her if she could not speak good English. It seemed like her family and the people they talked to, what Vater still called *unser leighte*, were being left behind, because when they went to a town there it was German and English, too, but the English was very quick and contained more words than she had. She would have to wait for a boy who liked to speak only German, if there was such a one.

She pulled the milk from the cow's teats steadily, one-two, one-two, squeeze-relax, squeeze-relax, quitting only when the last drops came. If the cow was not milked dry then the mastitis would come, thick, stinking strings of infection plugging up the teats and hardening the udder so the milk could not come, and if it got bad enough the cow would never milk again and maybe die. There were many such things to worry about. Sometimes it seemed the animals were just waiting for somebody to make a tiny mistake so they could die.

And it was not only animals that would die from a mistake. Even the fresh milk, Selma knew, which looked so clean and tasty to drink, had to be taken care of carefully. Some of it went to feed the young pigs, so that was easy. Just carry it to the wooden troughs, pour it in, and stand back. It was gone in seconds, but even then the troughs soaked up a little so they were always smelling sour.

Some of it had to be set in the ice-house right away so it would not sour, and that much must be kept perfectly clean. In winter it was easier because the weather was always cold and there was no mud or dust to drop into the buckets. But bad milk could bring milk fever, and from that people would die.

But tonight Mutter would take care of the milk because Selma had other chores yet to do. "Come, Henry," Selma said when she had finished the second cow. "We must clean up around the threshing machine again." Henry pouted for a minute. He was proud to be helping if it was man's work, but this was the sister again.

They walked out to the field where the threshing machine was, Selma thinking that Martha should be with them, but that could never be.

The third stack was a quarter mile from the barn, next to some wild plum bushes and scrub poplars in the ravine where the beef cattle could get shelter from the winter wind. The two stacks in the barnyard were for bedding in the barn, for the pigs to live in, and for shelter for the milk cows when they were outside.

The land rose gently just before the ravine, and on the high spot Selma stopped to look around at the shallow, rolling hills still green in the pastures and wild lands, but golden where there was grain, and black where fields were kept in summer fallow. Whenever she could she came to this place to look away from the farm, far and away where so many strange places and people were. She could see other familiar farmsteads, one where the bachelor newcomer Johann Flagan lived just a half-mile away to the south, another perhaps two miles off, the home of Martin Seibern and his parents. And there were more, she knew, all across the prairie, but in all the distance there was no noise and nothing was moving except the grass with the wind.

After a while she knew she was wasting time and walked on down to the machinery and the strawstack.

In winter the pigs would burrow out of sight into the stacks, and when Vater called "Po-o-i-ig, po-o-i-ig" they would burst up out of the straw, snuffling and squealing, and come to the trough for their grain. The cattle ate caves all around the edges of the stacks if they did not get enough hay to keep them full, but mostly they lay at night in the deep, loose straw the pigs had dug up. Sometimes a cow would step on a buried pig and there would be shrieking as bad as when one was caught for butchering. By spring the stacks looked like giant mushrooms.

The sun was going down soon so Selma and Henry would not have long to clean up. The grain spilled from holes worn in the sheet-metal sides of the machine, or shook loose from the bundles before they went into the machine. There was never much from this, and it would not be clean grain because they were picking by hand and getting plenty of chaff and dirt with it, but Vater said nothing should be wasted, and the chickens didn't seem to complain that they were not the best grain getting.

It was nice to be out away from the housework, away from the heat of the summer kitchen. The breeze kept down the flies and mosquitoes, and Henry talked only a little. Their voices disappeared quickly in the quiet of the distances.

"Come on now, start picking," Selma called. She held her apron pinched together with one hand to hold the grain and carry it to a sack near the machine. Henry helped a little bit, scooping two hands where there was a little pile easy to get, but when it came to picking up single grains he lost patience and wandered off by himself.

Selma did not mind. She was tired and did not want to argue with him. And tomorrow the machine would lose more grain, so they would have to do it again, and if that was the last day they could finish the whole thing then. But that wandering off could be the danger, too, so she kept an eye on him. It had cost them Martha.

The first time the machine had come it had frightened Selma, it was so big and so loud. It roared and it shook, and the whirling knives where the men threw in the grain bundles looked like giant claws. In fact, they were terribly dangerous, she knew, and even though the men got used to working right on top of them all day long, they feared that part of the machine more than anything, and they took no chances with it. It could chop a man in pieces as easy as it did a bundle of grain.

And the steam engine was no better, with a roaring all its own, and the huge flywheel driving the long whining belt to the threshing machine with power that could snag a man and whip him like a rag doll back into the wheel where he would lose an arm or a leg, or his life.

It was dangerous for the horses, too, because they had to pull the wagons up alongside the machinery and sometimes if they were frightened they bolted and ran blind, perhaps into the flying belt, knocking it off its drive wheel, but not before they were horribly burned and cut.

But the machinery was better than a hundred people for threshing the grain out of the straw, Vater always said. "Jah, we had nothing like this monster in Deutscheland," Johann Flagen had said. "Dangerous but better than by hand."

And the machine was pleasing to Vater, too, Selma knew, because he wanted to be the best farmer, wanted to make money. "Some risk and some noise for a few days," he said. "But so fast and so cheap for so much more grain."

She bent beside the silent gray monster and picked for a time, but after she emptied her apron once into the sack she stood doing nothing, looking at the reds and blues of the sunset, feeling the breeze on her sweaty forehead, thinking it was fall coming, and the air was as if it was waiting for something.

She thought again that they were all waiting for something. Vater was waiting each year for the planting, the haying, the grain harvest, the troubles of winter, the spring and the next planting, and for the land to make him rich. Mutter was waiting for just a little more money from the crops so the house could be bigger, or so that Vater would finally buy a decent coat, or best of all so that she could have real cupboards and a bigger space for cooking. Ludwig was waiting to farm only his own land. Emily was waiting to marry the man, Martin Seibern, and leave home. Henry was waiting to be a man.

And Selma is waiting for what, she thought. To be married, too? She remembered asking Mutter what it was to marry, and she laughed to herself at what she had thought then. Being married was not so simple as to have a friend. There was more, things that happened in a bed. Selma tried not to think too much about that, though she understood some of it. The bull and the cows, the roosters and the hens, the boar and the sows, and the stallion, which a man brought in the spring to the mares…nothing could be plainer after a while. And the men laughed at such things and told stories, too, when they thought the women did not hear.

She had asked Mutter once and been told sharply, "We don't talk about that." Selma had left the kitchen but then come right back for something and been surprised to see Mutter laughing to herself, and…when she saw Selma…blushing.

Maybe that was what women were supposed to be waiting for, Selma had thought, but she thought, too, that her understanding when she was ten had been better. Being married would be to have a friend, someone she could talk to besides Emily—who seemed older—and Mutter, who was too busy.

The ground was dusty and bare near the machine, stamped down by two days of the men's boots, the horse hooves, and the wagon wheels. But farther away from the machine the oat stubble was still standing thick. Henry was out into the stubble, and Selma thought she should call him back and put him to work, but she still didn't move, looking off in the evening and thinking about what it would be like to have a friend to talk to, but knowing it was more than the talking, someone who would smile at her when she smoothed her summer dress over her figure.

"Selma! Selma!" she heard Henry call, and she jumped with fear. In her mind she could smell the smoke of the stubble Ludwig had been burning, could hear Martha's screams as her dress caught and she stood tiny and stiff in the flames, her hands raised as if they should not burn, the fire quickly reaching to her hair.

It had been years ago, when Selma was six and would have burned, too, but she was not quite so far into the stubble playing.

"I caught a mouse," Henry said. "Want to see it?" He was holding out one hand.

"Keep your filthy mouse," she said, and he laughed and left her alone. Selma felt weak, confused for a moment.

What should she have done? She had been only six. But the grain sacks had been beside the threshing machine as they now were. The buckets of water had been beside the steam engine. She could have grabbed a sack, soaked it in the water, slapped down the flames on Martha.

Instead, she had stood screaming herself, but was safe on the packed ground, crying as her sister fell—a blackened horror.

Only fifty yards, maybe less. Something could have been done. Martha's screaming was still in Selma's ears, an inhuman sound, worse than the pigs when a cow stepped on them.

Ludwig had come on the run and carried Martha to the house, the whole time shouting, "Get Mutter! Get Mutter!" though Selma had fallen far behind him. By the time Selma got to the house, her breath had come short and raw in her throat, Ludwig had already laid Martha's naked, skinny body on the bed. Selma was frightened seeing the blackened body against the white sheets.

They had pulled the rest of the burned cloth from Martha's skin and washed her with cool water. Halsey's Burn Ointment was supposed to heal burns but there was only enough for the face, and for the rest of her they had only lard. The legs were the worst, but all over her the skin was blistered, some of it black even after washing, even in her mouth. Her hair was gone and her scalp burned, too.

"Don't look," Mutter had finally told Selma. "Go outside and pray for Martha."

And even that I didn't do, Selma thought, *because I didn't know any words for prayers about people who burned up.*

For two days in the house there was nothing but caring for Martha. Selma was not allowed to see her sister again, but she could hear the moaning sometimes and the strangling sounds in the throat. In the third night Martha gasped a bit more and died, and though no one ever said such a thing to Selma, she had gone on feeling as if she had done something wrong.

This evening she could not bear to be on this spot anymore. She was thinking of Martha too much. Vater would want the work done but if he was angry with her she would tell him plainly she was remembering Martha. That he would understand, because he and Mutter and Ludwig were all thinking the same as Selma about it, but not talking. She knew they were. And it had to be worse for Ludwig, who had been only fourteen but doing a grown man's work burning the fields, yet too young to be thinking about what could happen to the younger ones always, and Martha dead because of that.

She called Henry back from the stubble. "We don't have time to finish tonight," she said. "But I have enough for the chickens. Back to the house we go."

1906

Selma was seventeen and she still liked to stand on the rise above the buildings, looking across the distances, wondering what her own life was to be and waiting for it to begin. At the same time it was still painful to be there because just down in the ravine she thought she could still see Martha burning, still hear the screams of the tiny voice.

Eleven years pass, and now there are two, she thought on this day.

She had a shovel and was digging a hole in the dry ground. Ludwig was coming to help pretty soon with a bar for the harder soil or if they hit rocks, but so far each time Selma pushed down with her foot she was still making progress. She was surprised at how slow it went, how big a hole had to be for a man's grave.

Sometimes even now, thinking about Martha left Selma aching in her throat until she could hardly breathe. Mutter seemed to know when it was that bad. She would hold Selma for a little and say, "Try not to think about it."

Other times Mutter would say, "Get busy and do something to keep you from thinking about it."

That seemed to be what Mutter did. Shut it out. Work, work, work. Not very often did she talk about Martha, nor about any troubles for that matter, and when she did she was not sounding so sad as it felt to Selma. But Selma thought that maybe at night, maybe when Mutter thought no one else was in the house, the sadness must happen to her as it did to

Selma, because Mutter could not always hide the sounds of her own crying.

For Vater it had been even worse. For a couple of years he pretended to go along the same, working as hard as ever, cheerful for everyone, but after a while even the children could see the tiredness begin to take him. His black beard turned gray, his shoulders seemed to become smaller, and he did not wash himself for weeks.

"Did you feed the pigs? Did you get water to the cows? Aren't you going to finish plowing the east field?" Mutter would ask him every day. She had come to know that he forgot things, or just did not do them, so she kept up the questions and pushed the unfinished work onto the children or herself.

The only time Mutter seemed to sit still and be calm was when she was in church. There Selma tried to be the same, singing the hymns, some now so familiar she did not need the book for them, hearing the pastor speak of sin and death and forgiveness and life everlasting, of the power of the devil and the goodness of God.

Getting to church took time, and they could not go every Sunday, but when they did there was always one hymn from Martin Luther they sang:

"A mighty fortress is our God,
A bulwark never failing,
Our helper He amid the flood,
Of mortal ills prevailing.
For still our ancient foe,
Doth seek to work us woe,
His craft and power are great,
And armed with cruel hate,
On earth is not his equal."

Selma loved that one because it was best for men's voices and for that one the men would join in finally, making the music strong. But she tried not to think too much about the meaning of it, because it seemed God had forsaken them when Martha died. She could only think it had been a punishment for something they had done, something she didn't know about.

She knew a few more hymns by heart, the first verses at least. On summer days she liked one that said:

When morning gilds the skies,
My heart awak'ning cries,
May Jesus Christ be Lord,
When evening shadows fall,
This rings my curfew call,
May Jesus Christ be praised.

Vater only knew one by heart, and he would sing it loud over and over, off-key.

"Fear not, though faithful Christian flock," he would roar, *"God is thy shelter and thy rock."*

Selma thought it was, to him, a song about *unser leighte*.

When he sang Mutter said nothing but she made sure he could see her covering her ears as the children did to him. But the last few years he had not sung very much at all.

Mutter knew many hymns by heart and would hum or sing them all day as she worked. But lately Mutter had not been singing so much either, except for one which Selma did not like:

O, Paradise, O Paradise, Who doth not crave for rest?
Who would not seek the happy land, where they that loved are blest...

And now there are two, she thought again as she dug. And now she knew why Mutter had been singing that unhappy song.

The punishments were too much. If God was truly the helper amid the flood of mortal perils, He needed to do something now, something to help carry the loss of Vater.

She was sweating hard, and knee-deep down in loam and sand she hit some hardpan clay. The shovel began skipping off when she stamped it, so she stopped and sat on the edge of the hole for a time. Ludwig was coming up the hill with the pointed bar. Selma felt guilty for thinking God was not helping enough.

"Is it all done?" Ludwig asked, trying to make a little joke.

He had grown taller than Vater, or maybe it was that Vater had shrunk shorter in the last year. He kept a mustache and always wore a hat, and he was strong from working so much in the fields since he was little. The bar was heavy and long, but Ludwig could take it in two hands and easily slam it six inches into the clay. He worked steadily, loosening the clay in chunks and shoveling it out.

"What is going to become of us?" Selma asked. "What will we do without Vater?"

She was remembering the time she had read to Vater about the $28 Russian coat, when he had held her in his lap and they had all been happy. It hurt so much to remember, hurt just like when she thought about Martha.

But it was the future, the farming, that she was worried about without Vater. Somebody had to do the work, somebody had to pay the bank after the harvest.

"Mutter has a plan," Ludwig said between shovelfuls. "She will run the farm."

"She has told you this? She tells me nothing," Selma said.

"Just this morning she told me," Ludwig went on. "She has been up all night. She will tell you when she can."

He shoveled some more. "Vater has not been much good for a long time," he said after a while. "I think Mutter has been planning for much longer than last night."

Leaning her hands and chin on her shovel handle, Selma stood back away from the hole and watched Ludwig dig. He had already deepened it enough that he was in up to his hips. "Yah," he said, "and I think she will make it work. I will help, and Henry is twelve, he will soon do a man's work, and maybe there will have to be a hired man sometimes. And Emily and Martin, but not much there, I think, when Emily has babies. And you."

"The bank will have something to say," said Selma. She did not keep the books. Vater had done that, but she and Mutter had talked about it with him from time to time. Every year there was borrowing and paying back, borrowing and paying back, and not only from the bank. Selma did not know if that was bad or good, but it seemed something Mutter and Vater worried about all the time. The bank, the bank.

"Yah, but the crop looks good for this year. This winter will be nothing to worry about. In the spring…if the bank will loan to a woman, that is different. But maybe to me if they will not. There must be money for seed and machinery parts and some new harnesses we need."

"So I must help out, too," Selma said.

Ludwig stopped digging, straightened, and looked at her. "If you get married you must leave then," he said. "You must have your own life. I know that. Mutter knows it."

Selma thought about Wilbur, Wilbur Metwald, who had a quarter section of his own and a poor house, who had spoken to her a year ago when he was on the harvest crew, and who had been courting her since spring. He was tall, taller than anyone in Selma's family, and rough talking, and four years older. At first she had been proud a grown man would court her, excited that she would have someone not of the family to talk to. A friend, before the other things would come into it.

But his talking was only about his farm and about needing a wife to help him. He brought her flowers and took her for rides in a borrowed buggy, and more than once they had kissed and she felt herself warming to him, but he did not press her yet for anything like the men told stories about. When he had started visiting her Mutter had told her straight out, "Do not shame yourself. Men are men. You must not give in to them." Since Wilbur had not been trouble that way yet, she thought he must be a good man.

Still, he was not a friend like the picture she had in her mind. He did not talk about…about Selma and Wilbur. Only about the farming and money, and sometimes bragging about drinking beer and always about getting the best of the deal when he bought a cow or horse.

She had to be grown up. A friend was something from her childhood. If she was to marry Wilbur it would be for helping, a helpmate as the Bible said, and for rearing children. The farm must come first, that she understood, though the idea of a friend was hard to put away. Mutter and Vater had been such friends.

Not so much this past two years, though. Something there had died before this summer.

"Vater had been sick much longer than he told us," Ludwig said. "And Mutter knew it, too. Maybe as far back as Martha. Mutter did not want to talk about it, but she has been thinking for a long time."

He went back to his digging. "You will have to read from the Bible when we are burying him," he said, his voice muffled from down in the hole. "The pastor, we cannot get quick enough."

No time to get a pastor, Selma knew, though the family had discussed it. But Vater had died just yesterday, and Mutter said there was not money enough for an undertaker and a headstone, so the burial must be at home, and that meant today. She had walked to Emily's place two days ago to tell her, Emily, to come say good-bye, and Martin Seibern had ridden to tell Ludwig, and that was all there would be.

For keeping the body they had spread sand on the front room floor, and had rags soaked in rubbing alcohol. Mutter said she could not bear to touch Vater again. "The dead have certain ways..." she had said to Selma, and she made the sign of the cross. So Selma had been the one to roll him over, soak the rags, roll him back. She was sick with missing him already, but she would not miss that job, and she wondered what ways the dead had, and what would become of her because she had touched him.

"Maybe I will read about the land of milk and honey," she said.

Ludwig chuckled from below. "He would say you are making a joke at his funeral. Instead you should find something about going back to the homeland. That he would like."

"I don't know if there is that in the Bible."

"Well, that is what the land of milk and honey is about. Maybe there is nothing else. I guess you will have to read it after all."

"Ludwig, do you think this is the land of milk and honey?" she asked, looking around at the familiar prairies, feeling a dampness in the air for the first time in weeks. She shivered once as the sweat cooled on her and she wished she had brought her sweater.

"It is land. That is all I know. And we must have land. How else do people live without land?"

That was a question. How did people live without land? And how would the family live if they lost this land, if the bank would not loan, if the women could not get the crops in and the animals fed in winter. How would they live?

It was frightening to think about.

There had been letters from Retzlaffs and Flegels still in Russia, and in the last year the letters held stories of people with no more land, no more crops, sent away from their home villages with no place to go. Some were still trying to come to America. Some had disappeared. There was trouble with something called Bolsheviks and Mensheviks. Some Germans were still in the villages writing: *Things will get better, God will provide*, but in the next part writing: *We are so poor, so hungry*.

Whenever Selma heard about it she was so glad Vater and Mutter had left there, and she knew Mutter was, too. "When you hear about Russia, leftovers in North Dakota are fine," Mutter would say.

But what direction would they go if they had to leave the farm? East? West? North? South? It was all the same…gentle hills and fields and fields, someone else owning all of it, strangers mostly, and even if there was a place to go, how would they get there? Towns, yes, but what did people do to live in a town? And it would be shameful to move in with relatives. And they did not have wagons to move everything. And horses could only pull a few days and needed rest, and where would that be? And harnesses could break, and there could be runaways if the horses saw a train or a tumbleweed…

Mutter was right. She had to keep the farm. Anything else was too big, too frightening.

Maybe Wilbur Metwald would be something safe for Selma. When she thought about no land, no place to go, having something safe seemed more important than having a friend.

After a while Ludwig rested again. Now he was in to his waist. He shook his head. "Mutter is strong," he said. "So strong. Do you know she is going to homestead more land?"

"She can do that?"

"Yes. She says she must get more in case there is trouble on this farm. She says we will only do what the law says to prove up the land, so we do not need every year to farm it. That would be too much work for anyone. But she wants more. And I think she is right. She and Vater had talked about it, but Vater told her he could do no more."

"If the bank…"

"Always 'if the bank,'" Ludwig said.

Selma thought for a time. "Perhaps Wilbur Metwald can help, too," she said with an idea.

"No. It must in the family stay."

He looked up at her, saw she was hurt.

"Only because if it is lost, it should be on us, no one else," he said.

Selma wondered if it was that, or something else with Wilbur Metwald. She knew Mutter did not like the man but said nothing. And Ludwig would never speak of such things.

The sky was slate gray and a wind was picking up. Selma's dress was swirling against her legs and she shivered some more. Rain would be coming, maybe not today, but soon. After that…harvest time.

And without Vater's help.

If they got the harvest in, that would mean it could be done. Maybe Mutter could keep it going without Vater, but for sure not alone. No one could do all of it alone. There must be a hired man or two, and Henry more and more, and Ludwig must come back to the home farm as much as he could.

Because Selma herself had to leave. Perhaps not this winter, but she had been waiting for a long time for something, someone, for her own life to start, and now that would be with Wilbur. She could make a life with him. She could help Mutter, too, for a time yet, but not for always.

There must be something for me, she thought.

Chapter Three

November 1914

Any time the travel was away from home, the little white horse Kurtzie, Shorty, was a cheat. She would let the other one do all the pulling if she could, walking back just enough to keep the tugs slack. Selma had hooked the tug-chains one link shorter to keep her pulling, but Kurtzie had figured that out, too, long before they'd made the 14 miles to Kulm, and would have been cheating some more if Selma hadn't constantly slapped her rump by popping the driving line. By the end of the trip, Selma's left arm had felt limp like a dishrag.

The other horse, a huge black gelding, did not cheat no matter what. After one look at his over-sized, bulge-nosed head no one ever asked about his name—Schnauze, the Nose. He was so ugly Selma felt sorry for him, and so good to pull she could always depend on him. Yet she dreaded harnessing him because he was so tall she could barely get the harness on, a struggle each time. With her right arm she would throw the harness as high as she could, trying to get the off-hame over the horse's back instead of just stabbing him in the ribs, and then pushing the forty pounds of slipping straps up and back before they all slithered down in a heap at her feet and she would have to start over. She was glad Schnauze stood for it.

Kurtzie, a good eight inches shorter, should have been easy to harness, but she would not stand still, so she was a struggle, too, and Selma had to watch all the time so the shifting horse wouldn't plant a hoof right on Selma's toes.

Now, heading home, they made better time because cheating Kurtzie was good to pull, too, when she was headed toward the familiar barn.

Selma was worried about the cow, which hadn't been milked since yesterday morning, and the pigs, which had no food today. The cow would be bawling and the pigs so hungry they'd be squealing and ramming each other around with their snouts, but it couldn't be helped. Going to town was two days, and with Wilbur gone no one could be home to milk and feed, and neither Ludwig nor Henry could come over.

She had decided on the farm wagon even though there was some snow on the ground. The wind blew the road bare in some places, so if she had hitched to the bob-sled there would have been the grinding noise and the harder pulling as the runners went on the dirt. There were enough drifts to worry her when the wagon went across them, but so far they had not got stuck, and they were getting close to home.

Rudolph and Daniel, aged six and four, were big enough to jump around in the wagon and stay warm, and sometimes they got out and ran alongside to warm up some more. Still they complained, and Selma didn't want to scold them for it. She was cold, too, from the sitting still on the hard seat, and the wind.

They plodded south on the frozen road that climbed and dropped on the contours of the hills, snow firmed on the slopes facing north, but melted away to bare dirt on the slopes facing south. The sun was shining between snow squalls, but all day the wind moved delicate veils across the road from west to east, right on the ground no higher than the horses' knees. Sometimes it played tricks on the eyes, looking like the whole earth was moving sideways.

Selma remembered when she was in school, the children laughing about covered wagons. A grandma's bonnet pulled by horses. But right now that bonnet would feel good, because at least the children could sit in back and not have the wind hitting them. This open wagon was nothing for shelter, and with no springs under it, nothing for comfort either.

The children had plenty of clothes on for the weather if they weren't sitting still, but of course there was too much sitting. Selma herself wore two pair of woolen mittens, but the wind still cut through them, and a long coat, a woolen sweater over her dress, a muffler wrapped around on top of her scarf, and she kept the blankets wrapped tight around her feet because overshoes were never enough against the cold unless you happened to be walking hard.

Rudy complained most, every few minutes, saying, "Mama, I'm freezing. Mama, I'm freezing."

Selma tried to keep him occupied by each time telling him something different. "Jump around in the back again," she would say, or "Jump out and run along with us," or "Come snuggle in the blankets with me." When they came alongside a pasture she told them, "Count the posts," though neither boy could count past ten yet, or when they could see a farmhouse in the distance she said, "Tell me a story about who lives there." But none of it worked for long.

What she really wanted to tell him was, "Just be quiet and suffer. That's what I am doing."

She worried most about little Christina, because Christina could only move around in the back and not much of that because she might fall out. The rest were just sitting under the blankets, and five or six hours of that was too much for a child of two, and she was so young she would not know to warn Selma if she was getting frostbit.

Not a trip for children, Selma thought. But it was almost winter, and salt they must have, and baking powder, beans, matches, coal, kerosene, some wheat ground for flour, and more, much more than she had had money for.

The clerk had seemed nervous about telling her. "It is time to pay the bill," he had said, looking away behind her. "You have too much on credit, and I have bills to pay, too."

Selma had been embarrassed because she knew what he would say before he said it, and she did not like to be in debt to him. But she had so little money, and the rooming house for overnight was only cash.

41

"I am sorry," she told the clerk. "But Mr. Metwald is not yet back from shipping the cattle, and I must have these things. We will pay the bill as soon as he comes home."

That wouldn't have been so bad but there were other women in the store listening to it. They had turned away, pretending not to hear, but the store was small.

"I'm sure I will not be the only one happy to see Mr. Metwald," the clerk had said to make matters worse. For a moment Selma had wanted to snap back at him. What was it against her that Wilbur was not back? It was against him, Wilbur, who had stayed too long and left her with the work and the bills.

But she could not take a chance that the clerk became angry and sent her away. So she took it from him, wanting to run out she was so embarrassed.

The longer she watched the rumps of the horses and the snow moving in front of them the more angry and worried she was, because now the clerk had forced her to say it to herself. Wilbur should have been back three weeks past, maybe more.

Chicago was a distance she did not understand, nor did she know how long it took a cattle train to get there, nor how long to make the sale and turn around for home. But it had been the first week of October when the farmers put together a herd and drove it to Edgeley to load on the train. Wilbur had sent eleven head himself, big fat steers a year-and-a-half old and worth good money, and then with two other men he had gone along to keep an eye on the cattle and make the sale for everyone.

He should have been back, no matter how far it was.

"Will Papa be home when we get there?" Rudy asked her. He was sitting with her in the blankets again.

"I don't know," was all she answered. "But soon he will be home."

Not soon enough. Already Rudy was figuring out that without Wilbur at home he, Rudy, could be unruly because Mama was too busy to keep track of him. So she had caught him slapping the tied-up milk cow with a stick, making it jumpy to handle at milking time, and when Selma told him to bring buckets of grain to the pigs he just ignored her until she was shouting at him, and one day picking eggs he broke them

42

all, throwing them at the wall, and he had blamed it on Daniel.

He was afraid to do those things with Wilbur, who would spank him for it, maybe with a razor strap. Once when Rudy was three Wilbur had struck him with fists. Selma tried not to think about that time.

"Grandma's house," little Daniel said, pointing down eastbound wagon ruts. "I want to go Grandma's house get cookies."

"Turn, Mama. Turn," Rudy said, jumping on the idea. "We can go to Grandma's and get some cookies."

Selma would have liked to go to the home place herself, but the milk cow couldn't wait. She would have liked to go there and say, "Mutter, watch the children while I sleep for a while. Mutter, Wilbur has not yet come home from Chicago with the money. Mutter, I am worried that Wilbur is playing cards someplace again and losing the money…again. Mutter, Wilbur has been a husband, but not a friend, and I have no one to talk with, and I am sick with loneliness. Mutter, I have not been in a church for a year. Mutter, the work is too much and Wilbur is all big talking but we are not getting ahead. Mutter, I have three children in six years, and without Wilbur home I am already having trouble making Rudy obey, and Christina is all day sitting on the floor with nothing to do when I am working, and Mutter, I need help with it."

Ach, she thought when she said it to herself. *So now you feel sorry for yourself.*

"We must go home," she told the children. "Another day we go over to Grandma. Maybe Uncle Ludwig or Uncle Henry will come take us in a buggy so we don't have to go with pokey old Kurtzie and Shnauze. Should we sing for a while?"

"I'm freezing," said Daniel. "But cookies warm you up."

"I don't want to sing," Rudy said. "I want some cookies."

"Well, I don't have any cookies," Selma said. She was down to her last trick, but she was getting close to home, too. "But maybe some candy would help?"

"Candy," Christina's tiny voice piped from under the blankets.

"In the crate with the beans," Selma told Rudy. "Bring me the little sack."

She turned to watch Rudy rummage in the back of the wagon. He had to hang onto the side with one hand because the wagon swayed and bumped with the roughness of the road. Selma's back was hurting from twisting and jarring so much, and she thought again the bob-sled would have been much smoother.

Just as she thought, Rudy would have sat there and eaten the candy by himself. "Bring it to me or I will stop and spank you," she had to tell him.

First there were chocolate squares, two each, but these disappeared quickly. Then she gave them hard candies to suck on. Each might last a half a mile or better, she thought. Three or four each. Then they would be home.

Kurtzie and Schnauze knew it, too, and they were walking briskly, sometimes breaking into a jog, but even though she wanted to hurry Selma could not let them do that because the ride would be rougher yet.

The horses ears pricked forward as they saw their own turn-off coming up, but it wasn't only the barn that had them interested. Coming up the road in front of her, maybe a half-mile away, a covered buggy pulled by a single horse. She could see it was making good time, the horse at a long trot, the buggy swaying and pitching softly. It was enclosed all around, with isinglass windows front and back and the driving lines going through the dashboard.

Springs under it, Selma thought enviously. And the wind shut out.

She didn't need to tug the left line to turn her own horses because they knew the way. Now the ride was even rougher as the wagon jarred in and out of ruts, no built-up road at all, but it was only a quarter-mile to the house and at least the wind was at their backs. Almost to the buildings she turned to see how far the buggy had gone and was surprised to see it had turned in and was following her. In the yard she halted the horses at the gatepost near the house, got Christina down and told her to run and play. "Daniel, keep an eye on Edith," she said. "And both of you run around and get warm."

It would be dark soon enough, and the house would be cold. "Bring some coal to the stove," she told Rudy, and before he ran off she took his shoulder and said again, "Bring in some coal. I mean it. We must get the house warmed up. You get the coal and let the other two play."

The driver of the buggy pulled near to the barn instead of the house. Before he stepped down Selma could see him pushing aside a thick robe. He took a weight from the buggy, set it in front of the horse, clipped the halter rope to the weight. He seemed in no hurry, blanketing the sweaty horse and buckling a feedbag on its nose before approaching the house.

Selma didn't know who it was and she was a bit anxious. He was not a big man but he seemed sure of himself, as if he had been on this place other times. He wore a long coat and a flat hat, and when he approached he tipped the hat and asked, "Mrs. Wilbur Metwald?" At the same time he pulled back the coat and Selma could see a badge shining on his shirt pocket. "I am Dickey County Deputy, William Bauman," he said in English.

Selma felt her heart begin to speed up even before her mind began to frighten her.

"Yes, Selma Metwald," she answered, and then the fears caught up to her. The bills had not been paid. The bank, the bank…she had on purpose avoided the bank when she had been in Kulm.

Or something with Wilbur.

For a second she felt like the earth was slipping away in front of her, as it had seemed to be doing with the ground blizzards she had been staring at all day.

"Is Mr. Metwald at home?" The deputy looked at Selma as he spoke, but she could see that he was also looking the place over and she was ashamed of it…the unpainted barn with bawling cows and pigs wandering through it, the barnyard with manure piles that should have been hauled to the fields last spring, the field machinery parked here and there with little snowdrifts against them and nothing parked in a straight row, the patched-up gates and outhouse with broken door, the single-story house with no paint either, and one window blocked with a blanket.

"No, he is with the cattle to Chicago," Selma answered.

"That was some time ago, I believe," the deputy said, and waited.

"Yes. He should be any day home now."

Selma's feet were numb with the cold. She wondered if she should invite in the deputy, start the fire, make some coffee. She didn't want to stand out in the wind another minute, and no matter if she got the fire going she would still have to come back out for the milking and the feeding. She didn't know how to treat a deputy.

He seemed to be in no hurry. "You are certain Mr. Metwald is not at home?"

"I have heard nothing from him since he left," Selma answered. "And now I have since yesterday morning been to town, but he is not here. Can we go in? I must start the fire for the children. They are very cold."

"Yes, do that," the deputy said. "I'll take the feedbag off my horse and be in."

Selma started the fire in the front room by pouring a bit of kerosene on the fresh coal before she struck a match. She did the same in the kitchen stove with sticks of poplar, quick to burn up, but easy to start. She looked out the window and saw the deputy come out of the barn and go toward the outhouse before he came to the house.

He does not believe me, she thought. *He is looking in all the buildings.*

She did not know what to tell the deputy, but he was somebody to talk with. "Yah, I am worried about Mr. Metwald," she said when the children left. It was surprising to her that she would tell that to a stranger. "I think he should be back a while now."

"Can I look at the other rooms?" the deputy asked.

That startled Selma. So he still did not believe her.

"Yes," she answered, afraid to say no. "There is only the front room and the two bedrooms. And closets."

"And an attic?"

"Yah. The opening is in the closet."

She heard his bootsteps on the floors, and in a minute he was back. "I am sorry," he said. "It is part of my job to do that."

He said no more. Selma waited for him to speak, again not knowing what to say. Then she could stand it no longer.

"You have word from Mr. Metwald?" she asked.

The deputy sighed. "No, no word...not from Mr. Metwald." He

hesitated, sighed, pulled a paper from his coat pocket, and Selma could not stand the waiting. *Something bad,* she thought. *Something bad.*

"I must know what is happening," she said then. "Please."

"Not from Mr. Metwald. This is a telegraph from the Kulm bank to the sheriff in Ellendale. About the debts to pay this fall. And about the two men who went with Mr. Metwald to Chicago. They have been home at Edgeley since October 19th."

Selma stared at him, her heart pounding. She was not accustomed to looking an unfamiliar man in the eye but she couldn't help it. And as he looked back at her he didn't seem so frightening himself, it was more like pity, but that made the fear worse as she heard the message.

"The other men have been contacted, Mrs. Metwald. When they sold the cattle they all went to a saloon and did a little drinking, but the other two got on the train right back to North Dakota early the next morning. The last they saw of Mr. Metwald, he was still in the saloon playing cards."

"I have no money," Selma blurted out, and knew it was not the right words.

"If Mr. Metwald shows up, he must go to Ellendale to see the sheriff," the deputy said. "Or he can go straight to the bank in Kulm. And he should pay, or whatever the bank wants to do. It is only the bank's problem right now, but the sheriff has been contacted, so it must be cleared up. We are only looking for him for the bank, but we must know."

The children came in again. "We're hungry, Mama," Daniel said.

"Hungry, hungry," Christina repeated.

Selma had some bread a few days old, but not moldy yet. The butter was too hard to use so she broke up the bread in bowls and poured on some cream and a bit of sugar. "Take this in the bedroom and eat," she said. "But if you spill you will clean it up. Rudy, you take this one for Christina."

She had almost forgotten her manners. "You are hungry?" she asked the deputy.

He waved his hand. "No, no. I have plenty in my buggy, thank you."

"Coffee?" she asked. She was afraid of him, yet, afraid of what else

47

he might say, but she did not want him to leave. Coffee would take a while, first to boil the water, then to let the grounds settle.

"No thank you. I must be going." He stood, then sat down again. "You have help?" he asked. "Family?"

"Family three miles over," she answered. He was kind, not someone to be afraid of after all. "I cannot go there. The cattle here must be fed, and one is milking. And pigs we have, too."

"You have fuel and food?"

"Yah, maybe enough now for the winter since I have just come from town. And Wilbur will be back, I am sure. This makes me worry, but he will be back."

"And money?"

She hesitated. "A little. Not to pay the bank. Not the grocery bill."

"If he does not come back, you will lose the place," the deputy said, and then seemed to regret saying it. "I am sorry. I don't mean to make it worse."

"I know, I know," she answered. "The bank."

"Yes."

The deputy stood again. "I must go," he said.

"It is getting dark. You go to Ellendale?" It was a long ways, Selma knew. Much farther than to Kulm. A man in the house was not good, yet she did not want to be alone. "There are more blankets," she said. "And a couch in the front room."

He shook his head. "No, thank you," he answered. "I came up from Ellendale today, but I am only going eight miles now, to my parents' place. Then tomorrow I go back to my office."

"Eight miles?"

"It isn't bad. My road wagon has lanterns and I have a good horse. A little over an hour."

Eight miles in that fine road wagon. An hour. What a difference from two or three hours it would take jolting in the open farm wagon with Kurtzie and Schnauze.

When he had left Selma made some hot oatmeal for the children and ate some herself. It was too early for their bedtime but she tucked them in anyway. "Now you will be warm," she told them, and she made them repeat a bedtime prayer.

She unloaded the household goods from the wagon first, going in and out quietly, hoping the children would fall asleep but not trusting them to stay in bed. By the time she had finished, they had fallen asleep, so she left the rest of the supplies in the wagon and threw the tarp back over them. The horses were shivering from standing so long in the cold after working all day, and they pawed anxiously because they were hungry.

Selma lit a lantern, took it to the barn, came back and unhitched the horses from the wagon, drove them to the barn, unhitched the neck yoke and driving lines, so the horses were separated, led them into their stalls, wrestled off the harnesses and collars and hung them up. The milk cow bawled endlessly. *Do something to take your mind off of it,* Selma kept thinking, not sure if she was talking to the cow, or to herself.

She broke the ice in the water tank and took the horses back out there but they refused to drink. They hadn't had water since morning in Kulm, but she thought she could not force them. Tomorrow. She led them back to their dark stalls, tied them tight, fed a night's worth of hay.

The cow was next. Even though she wanted to be milked she was so full her udder was tender and she kicked twice as Selma washed her. The milk was dripping from the teats before Selma even got started, and it poured easily into the buckets. *No holding back tonight from you,* Selma thought. She left the cow tied instead of turning her back out for the night, and fed her hay as she had the horses.

Next were the pigs. They got most of the milk and some grain, enough to keep them happy until the next day. It was very dark now; she had to carry the lantern in one hand and so could only carry one bucket of feed or milk, slowing her work. She slipped sometimes on the packed snow of the barnyard, and twice she stubbed her toe on frozen piles of horse manure.

And the whole time she was asking herself, *What are you going to do? What are you going to do?*

That Wilbur. All his big talking about the deals he made, about what a big man he was with the farmers, all comes to this? A man who sits in the saloon and lets his farm and his wife and children be forgotten?

He would come home. He had to come home. No kind of a man would just walk away.

But what if he did not? What then?

He would come home. He had to come home. When he did she would tell him, too, and make his life miserable for what he was doing, even if he used his fists on her. Three babies he had made in six years, and he wouldn't make another one for the rest of his life, she would see to that if she had to sleep in the barn.

As soon as they had been married the nice talking had quit, and after that he only spoke what needed to be said. Six years she had tried to make his life pleasant even with all the work she had. Six years she had thought there might come a time when they might be…not friends, perhaps, not like Mutter and Vater had, but at least to visit, tease a little, laugh at something the children did.

Nothing had come of that. Her waiting for it was of no use.

But, still, what if he didn't come back?

The thought of it left her weak with worry, yet late in the night under all the blankets, finally warm but not sleeping a wink, she was surprised to find herself thinking if she could live without Wilbur it would be no worse than living with him, and for that she felt guilty, but later she was more surprised to find herself making plans.

Was this what it was like for Mutter when Vater died? Lay awake at night and figure it all out, then work like a plowhorse all day so you don't have to think about it?

She would like to have gone home to Mutter and asked how to do this, but she was twenty-five years old with three children. A grown-up. She had to do it herself.

She thought about how childish she had been to think about marriage as a way to have a true friend for herself, to have a boy admire her figure and smile at her in a new dress. What foolishness.

Twice she got up to check the covers on the children. Most nights Rudy thrashed around and lost his blankets. "You are running while you sleep," she would tease him. But not tonight. None of them moved.

Toward morning Selma dozed, but even in that she was thinking, and once half-awake came the word 'divorce,' and she was thinking that if he did not come back she was not going to live waiting for him. He would deserve to be divorced. *I will tell the children he was a schweinehund who deserted them and they cannot speak of him again. Divorce is a sin and I will never be forgiven, but if he has done this I will not be Mrs. Wilbur Metwald. I will not. I will be Selma Retzlaff only.*

She finally dozed off, only for minutes it seemed, until she heard Christina standing beside her saying, "Mama, hungry."

Selma bolted awake, confused, the word 'divorce' in her mind already.

We'll see about that, she thought when she was fully awake. *But first there are the children to feed, and the cow to milk, and the pigs to feed and bread to bake and the house is dirty and I must go and talk to Henry or Ludwig to come help me butcher.*

Get busy and do something so you don't think about it, she told herself.

March 1, 1915

Every day was the same. Selma got up well before the children, stirred up the coal fire and started a wood fire, ate a slice of bread with butter and jam, went out and gave Kurtzie and Schnauze some oats and more hay, milked the cow, and then was back in to feed the children.

She would eat some oatmeal with them or some bacon and more bread. Then she bundled them up and took them outside for some fresh air while she harnessed the horses and fed the pigs. Rudy was doing fine feeding the chickens and picking the eggs, though sometimes he was careless and left a few eggs to freeze. When the weather was too bad the children had to stay in and Selma took care of the chickens, too, and hurried back and forth from her work to the house to check on the children.

Only twice had the storms been so bad she could not go outside. Then for two days the animals went hungry, and Selma was tense and short-tempered worrying about it. But nothing had died yet.

The cattle had needed hay every day since early December except for a couple of days here and there when a warmer wind blew the snow off some hilltops. Most days Henry had been coming over after he fed

Mutter's cows and did the chores there. He came in a cutter and single horse straight across the prairie when there was good snow and the potholes were frozen, a shorter way than around by the roads.

Selma would help him hitch up her horses and pitch on a load of loose hay from the stacks in close to the yard. Henry would head out to the near pastures where the cattle were, letting the horses walk along by themselves while he pitched the hay off on the ground. Then he would go to the spring and chop away enough ice to show a trickle of water for the cattle, come back and put up Selma's horses, jump back in his cutter and go home for more work.

He was twenty-one and he was skinny. "Eat this, eat that," Selma told him. "Here is some sausage to chew on while you travel home."

He did eat all the time, everything that was in front of him, but he stayed skinny.

Now in March they were feeding from stacks a half mile from the barn, and Selma didn't want to leave the children home that long, so if the weather was too much for them to ride along Henry had to do it all. And it wasn't only the distance that took time. The stacks had settled so firm that before they could pitch the hay onto the sled, they had to cut away the day's feeding with hay-knives, like a sword with big round saw-teeth, heavy work and always watching not to cut off some toes at the same time.

There had been a few days of thawing and some of the snowdrifts were shrinking. The children had a sled from a cowhide dried raw with the edges curled up, and they used it to slide down the biggest drifts, especially the one on the north side of the barn which for a while had been above the eaves, partway up on the roof. When winter had started Selma had worried about how they would survive it. Now that it was March she worried how they would survive the mud when it came, especially when the cattle started calving and would still need hay hauled to them, and some would need help with the birthing.

Christmas Ludwig had come with a bobsled and taken them to Mutter's house. There had been few gifts for the children, some new mittens and caps that Selma had knitted late at night, shirts for the boys cut down from some of Wilbur's.

Selma thought at Christmas the only good thing so far was none of the children had been sick, and now in March she was still lucky that way. None of them anything more than the sniffles.

She herself was skinny, and strong, too, she thought. Like the horses. Every day the work. She fed the horses all the grain she dared so they could keep up, but she herself did not always feel like eating. Sleeping, yes. That she could have done.

Twice Henry had gone to Kulm in a cutter and brought mail and picked up groceries for Mutter and for Selma. When he took those trips he stayed with Selma the night before and used Schnauze to pull because the big horse was so faithful, and the cutter was so light it was nothing for him. When Selma sent Henry off she worried herself sick, and told him over and over, "Don't you dare get off the road for anything."

"Mutter tells me the same thing," Henry said. "And just as many times." He was taller than her and would reach over and pat her on the head. "Don't worry about me, little sister," he would say.

It made her laugh. He was the younger one. Sometimes Selma wondered what had happened to his childhood. She still thought of him as a child, helping to bury father, waving to his sister driving off with a new husband. It seemed so long ago yet it was like yesterday. She had been so busy having babies she had hardly noticed his growing up. When he had been two years boarding at high school she hadn't seen him then either.

But now he was a man, probably wishing he could live his own life instead of helping out his older sister and his mother. But he did not complain. He was so faithful and strong for her, like Schnauze but handsome, yet something of a stranger.

He did not complain about Wilbur Metwald, either, but he brought word from Kulm. No one had seen the man. No bills had been paid. The bank in Kulm was still interested in where Wilbur Metwald might be.

So Selma knew when the deputy drove in again what it was he would be talking about. He was driving a cutter instead of his road wagon, but like with the buggy he had lanterns mounted and heavy robes. The horse came right to the barn with that long trotting, smooth and quick and quiet, the only sound a faint squeaking of the iron runners of the cutter complaining against the snow.

Once again he took care of his horse with the blanket and nosebag before he came to the house. Once again he stamped clean his boots and took off his fur-lined winter hat. His mouth and jaws were hidden in a brown beard, his cheekbones red.

"Mrs. Metwald, you are well?" he asked.

"Yes. Fine. How do you do?" she answered.

"Fine, thank you. And your children?"

"They are well, too. Come in and sit."

So once again they sat across from each other at the kitchen table. *At least the room is warm this time*, Selma thought. *But still I shiver. What is it this time?*

"You have word of Mr. Metwald?" she asked.

"No. Nothing new." He shifted on the chair. "I am only stopping to check on you," he said. "I am coming from Ellendale again and going back tomorrow."

So what is it you want? Selma thought. *Are you just a kind man? Do you think you are going to come courting when the husband is gone? What is it?*

She did not trust him, but still she wanted someone to talk with.

Perhaps he read her mind. "My wife…my wife asked me to check on you," he said. "I told her about your situation last fall."

"She is kind," Selma answered, feeling foolish.

"Do you know what you will do yet? I am sorry to say it, but I don't think Mr. Metwald is coming back."

"I think he is not coming back, too," Selma said. "When I can travel with the children I will go in to Kulm and talk to the bank. That is first. Then…" she wondered if it was something she could ask a deputy, ask a man, "…how does a woman get a divorce? Do you know?"

Selma rose and went to the stove. "Coffee?" she asked. This time it would not take long because the water was already hot. "And I have bread fresh yesterday, and some jam from ground cherries."

"Yes. Thank you. That sounds good," he said.

He ate rapidly, like Henry, and sucked his coffee noisily like Wilbur.

But he said, "Excuse me," and Wilbur had never said that.

"Where will you go?" he asked then. "Relatives?"

"It is too difficult with my mother's place," she said. "My brothers do the work and they should not have more mouths to feed. I could go there but with three children...and my younger brother should be married and have his own family there. I don't know. I have nothing else but there is no place for me there, so that would be difficult."

She thought it would be something he might know. "Is there work in the towns?" she said. "I am strong, a good cook, farming, I can do anything."

The deputy shook his head. "I don't know of anything in Ellendale," he said. "And there are not many good houses to rent. If you went to a bigger town...Jamestown or Valley City, your chances would be better."

"I know no one there," Selma answered. The thought of going that far was frightening. She might as well go to Russia. "And no family to help when children are sick."

She thought about Rudy, still barely able to count, only knowing his ABCs, and old enough to be reading but he wasn't going to get that from her.

"If you should hear of something..." she said. "And I must be where the children can go to school."

He thanked her for the lunch. "I will wire to the banker," he said. "I will tell him it is something he should do quite soon." He laughed. "If he comes at all. I cannot arrest him if he doesn't want to travel."

She watched him pull the blanket off his horse, rub the horse on the shoulder, check the traces and drive off, the horse moving immediately into that swift trot, hooves flinging clods of snow back under the cutter.

So Henry and Ludwig are not the only kind men still alive in this world, she thought. *This deputy, too.*

For a minute she envied the man's wife, a woman she had never seen. Then she felt guilty. It was one of the Ten Commandments—"thou shalt not covet thy neighbor's wife" it said. That must mean something for women, too.

Still she could not help it, and the envy was in her mind mixed up with the anger she felt toward Wilbur, yet at the same time she knew it was a sickness in her heart, too, a hurtful thing that did not stop, that a man she had tried to be kind to, a man she had taken to bed and given three children, would not treat her kindly in return, but instead had run away for no reason she could understand at all.

March 6, 1915

Rudy had smashed some eggs again and this time Daniel did it, too. The chickens ate up the mess right away, but not only were the eggs gone, the chickens would start breaking eggs, too, once they had a taste. Selma was so angry. "When your father comes home…" she shouted at the boys, then stopped herself.

"When is father coming home?" Daniel asked as he had many times, and Selma was sorry she had mentioned the man.

She had quit lying to them with "Soon." They didn't believe her if she did say it. Little Christina said the word "Vater" when the boys mentioned him, but Selma doubted if the child really knew what the word meant. Five months Christina had been without a father and only two-and-a-half years old.

"He is coming home when he is coming home," Selma told the boys. "When he comes home we talk about it. Right now we don't talk about him. And don't you smash any more eggs. I will send you to bed without supper."

She wanted to spank them good, but it was cold enough out they were still wearing winter clothes, and spanking they would hardly feel.

Since the deputy had visited, Selma had been looking up the road every day for the banker, and when she saw a horse and cutter coming this morning, she was not surprised. It could be the deputy again, she thought, but he has nothing to stop here for, and the horse was not black, though it was tall and had the same long trot as the deputy's horse. The cutter was fancier, with red trim around the edges and a polished dashboard.

The traveler drove slower in the yard, stopping at the house gate. He saw Selma at the chicken house but didn't get out, instead waiting for her to approach the cutter. She wished she could have been in the house in a clean dress, but here she was in a dirty chores coat, woolen head scarf, overshoes, and Alfred's union suit under her dress. That he would not see, but she thought of it anyway.

"Mrs. Wilbur Metwald?" the man said. His legs were still under the buffalo robe. His coat was a black fur, sealskin Selma thought, with a wide collar turned up around his neck, and cap and mittens to match. He was a big man, red-faced from the wind, with a light mustache.

"I am Selma Metwald," she answered.

"August Weber," he said, and took off a mitten and extended his hand.

The banker, Selma knew this. She shook his hand, aware that her small hand was strong and calloused and cold within his huge, soft, warm fingers.

"Deputy Bauman tells me you have difficulty traveling," Weber said, speaking English. "And it is time we talk about things. So, I am here."

"It is good of you to come," Selma answered. "Come in. I will make coffee."

He was looking around at the place like the deputy had done, but Selma thought maybe not looking for Wilbur hiding. Looking for dollars.

Not much of that to see. No more than of Wilbur.

She seated Weber at the kitchen table, put on the coffee, and went to her bedroom where she got rid of the union suit, slipped on a clean apron, brushed her hair, and scrubbed her hands. The fingernails were broken and her callouses would not come clean, but it was the best she could do. She looked in the mirror, saw Selma still, not so old, thin, but with nice skin and big eyes.

Now I do not look like a barn maiden, she thought when she sat across from him. But in his eyes maybe she did. She tried to look at him directly, nervous but proud, too. Wilbur was gone since fall, yet she had lived almost to spring already with three children and all the work. Maybe this big, soft man could not have done it.

"I hope the winter has not been too hard on you," Weber began. She had expected something harsher, something…she wasn't sure.

Certainly this could not be another kind man in the world.

"We are here yet," she answered. "But I cannot go on another year like this."

"Yes, yes. It is too much for you, I am sure of that. And you know that there are debts to be paid."

"I do not know how much. Mr. Metwald did not tell me."

"Well, I have been asking some questions in Kulm. I hope you don't mind." He pulled a piece of paper from his vest pocket. "There is the grocery bill, $107. And the hardware and fuel $67."

"And the bank?" Selma asked.

"I will talk about that in a minute. There is more yet separate from the bank."

Selma held her breath and in her head she added.

"The livery stable $21. And at the implement dealer another $21 left on the mower."

"So…$216 this far," Selma said, and wrote with a pencil on a slip of paper.

"Yes. $216. Not so bad, but I am afraid none of these people will extend more credit for another year, not unless everything is paid up first. They…they know about Mr. Metwald. I don't think they will trust his name."

Selma nodded slowly. She would not have expected them to give her more. What she wanted more than anything was for something to happen so that she would not have to beg.

"And at the saloon, $34," the banker said.

Selma could feel herself getting angry. "That I will not pay," she whispered.

The banker chuckled. "I think the barkeep would expect you to say that. We'll leave that one for Wilbur Metwald."

He hesitated, and then asked, "Do you have any cash on hand?"

The children ran through the kitchen and out the door, no outdoor clothes on. "Excuse me, I must get them dressed for outside," she said.

It took her a while. Christina had wet herself and needed all clean clothes. She should have quit that by now but Selma had not had time to get her fully trained. "Get the sled and go sliding," Selma told them when she got them dressed. "I will come and get you when the man leaves. If you stay out I will make a surprise."

"I have not quite $40," she told the banker when she sat down again. "And I must have groceries soon again. So I cannot pay those bills."

"Your family can help?"

"I do not want to ask. They work hard and they are doing fine on their land, but these bills are not of them. These are of Wilbur."

"When the husband is gone the bills are on the place, or on the wife," the banker said. "I am sorry, but you cannot ignore them."

"I understand." And she did understand, but she had no plan for finding more money until they discussed the land and cattle.

"There will be plenty to pay these bills when we settle with the bank," Selma said.

The banker sat back and frowned. *He is trying to scare me,* Selma thought, *and he is doing it. But he will find out.*

"Well, okay. Let's talk about the bank. First there is $500 annual payment for the land purchase, three years remaining after this one that is overdue from fall."

Selma felt her breathing stop just for a second. Five-hundred seemed more than she could ever pay, and there was something wrong with his numbers.

"Wilbur tells me this is the last year," she said. "Since I was married, the land will be free and clear in 1915."

"I'm afraid Mr. Metwald re-mortgaged some time ago," Weber said. "The lien is against it until 1918."

And where did that money go? Selma wondered.

"So, $500 for one year, but $2000 until it is clear," she said. She was horrified at how fast it added up and angry that Wilbur had not told her everything.

"Yes. But there is also..." he looked at the piece of paper "...yes, $315 due at last harvest for farming expenses, including late payment penalty."

"That is the end?"

"Yes."

Selma added it all up. "So is it $2,531 for everything free and clear?"

He looked at his paper. "Yes. That is correct."

"And $1,031 would be for one more year only, but everyone paid up?"

"Yes."

Selma wrote some more, a list, and gave it to him. It read: 3 sows and 1 boar, 2 draft horses, 1 milk cow, 13 beef cows no gummers, 5 yearling heifers.

"How much?" she asked.

"What condition are they in?"

"Good. I have fed them well. The horses are strong. We work them all winter. The cows are healthy, almost to freshen now. Only one has a bad horn growing to her eye. And the sows are healthy, plenty grain they have been getting all winter, and all will have a litter soon."

Weber scratched around on his own paper for a minute. "The pigs I am not interested in," he said then. "I can only give you $20 for the lot of them. If the horses are good, $40 each. The milk cow $30, and all the beef together, $500."

"So...$630."

"Correct."

"I have perhaps 900 bushels of oats," Selma said. "Clean and dry. In sacks from harvest."

"That's good for $1 a bushel if I have to arrange to move it. A bit more if you haul it to town."

"So now we have $1,530."

"Yes. More than enough to pay everything for a year."

"But no horses to plow with."

"That is a difficulty for you. Yes."

"And no more grain to feed the animals."

"True."

"So I cannot sell all of it."

They were silent while Selma poured coffee for both of them. She was surprised to find that she did not mind this dealing with the banker, and she was no longer afraid of him.

"How much for the land?" she asked.

"Full quarter-section?"

"Yes. One hundred-sixty acres. Sixty acres cultivated, one spring, one well, two swamps. The rest pastureland…and one stand of poplar and a few elm and ash trees, perhaps five acres…and…the buildings…and the machinery."

He held the coffee cup almost daintily in his left hand, scribbling with his right.

"The buildings are not very interesting," he said.

"The house is good," Selma protested. "Small, and should be painted, and one window is out and the door broken a little. But you can see. Clean and no…" she could not think of the right English word, "…rottenness."

He looked around the kitchen. *His barn for that horse is probably better than this,* Selma thought.

"Yes, you're right. The house is not bad, if the floor is sound."

"It is good. It can be rented. Or built bigger. My parents lived in sod houses for many years coming from Russia."

I have nice skin, she thought, *and nice teeth. Why should I not smile at him?*

And she did smile. "A nice place for a young couple for starting out," she said.

And he smiled back. "I can see you have been thinking about this. I'm not going to best you in a deal, am I."

She smiled again, and then turned more serious. Not too much of that. "I hope you are not trying to best me," she said. "I am in a difficult place."

"But the best I can do is $8 an acre, buildings and all," he said.

Selma had not done much multiplying for a while, but she worked it out on the paper, hoping she would convince Weber he could not best her. "$1,280?"

"Yes."

Selma figured some more. "Is it $2,810 then for everything?"

"Yes. Well, there will be some taxes, too. That is not from the bank."

"I would have $279 for myself?"

"Yes."

She did not smile at him, but she did stare in his face for some time. She thought his round cheeks were turning more red.

"I have three children," she said then. "And nowhere to go."

"I am aware of that. But I have to…well…perhaps I could go to $10 an acre."

Selma figured some more. "I would have $599?"

"That sounds correct."

And she had $40 in her purse.

Six hundred and thirty-nine dollars, she thought. It sounded like a great deal of money, but where would more come from when that was gone?

"Twelve dollars an acre," she said then, wondering at her boldness.

"Mrs. Metwald…"

"And I must stay on the place until the weather is good," she said. "June or July?"

"Yes, you can stay. But if I find a sale for the land, or a renter, they will need to put in the crops. However, $12 an acre…I will give you $10. Nothing more. I could have you evicted and give you nothing and simply pay the taxes for a few years, and then I would own it. I am trying to be fair."

Now she was afraid of him again. She almost quit, but gave it one more try. "Ten dollars an acre and you pay up the taxes," she said.

He shook his head and didn't answer, and she thought she had gone too far.

"You are presenting me with some difficulties," he said. "But I want to be fair…"

He has difficulties? Selma thought. *He has difficulties? What does he know of that?*

But she didn't say it that way. "I am very sorry," she said. "But three children and a husband who leaves them…"

"Yes, I understand," Weber replied. "So I guess we can make that work."

Selma stood and reached out to shake hands with him. "Sold," she said.

Six hundred and thirty-nine dollars she would have.

He smiled broadly at her, but she still could not bring herself to smile at him again. Maybe she had done well, maybe she had been beaten. She did not know.

"You must come to Kulm and sign the papers," he said. "And I will give you a check then."

"If Mr. Metwald comes back…"

"Then our deal is off. Everything is in his name."

"And if he comes back after papers we have signed?"

"Then…he will have a hard time getting anything back from me. He will have to get a lawyer, go to court. He has abandoned everything. That is serious. I don't think a judge would give it back. I'm sure I can afford to fight it longer than he could."

She walked outdoors with him. The children were still sliding on the snowdrift. It was a nice day, trying to thaw.

Weber pulled the fur collar up around his neck, adjusted the robe on his legs, clucked to his horse. It turned a tight circle and the sun glistened off the polished surface of the cutter's dashboard, off the shining decorations on the polished harness.

Selma turned and went back into the house. There was a bit of chocolate left to make cocoa for the children.

She wondered if the banker's harness decorations were made from silver dollars.

March 15, 1915

After the banker's visit came two days of nice thawing with warmer wind from the southwest. The snowdrifts shrank down some more and bare patches grew on the higher ground. Then came more days of clouds and frost, snow squalls and gusting cold winds from the north.

Not spring yet, but no mud yet.

Selma was in the house kneading bread dough and watching out the window for the boys. They had gone out to the pasture to chase in a cow ready to freshen. Selma did not know if the cow would be chased or not, but the boys needed something to do, so she had sent them. The cow she would keep at the barn until it calved. The pasture was only the nearest one, less than a quarter mile from the barn, but Selma worried about the boys getting lost if a bad squall should come, worried that the cow might chase the boys. She hurried with the bread dough, patted it into baking pans, and set it near enough to the stove so it would rise.

"Come, Christina," she said then. "We must go out and help the boys get the cow."

If the cow would not come Henry would have to help with it, and he had enough to do without that. When the thawing came and the mud, he would not be able to get over to help her so much until the ground firmed up again. They had talked about it when they were pitching hay in the winter, and almost too late had decided to leave one stack near the barn so Selma could feed alone and without using the horses.

That stack had not been touched yet, but it was looking so small now. It might need to last three or four weeks, and if it did not, what then? Henry was already into the last of the stacks kept away from the buildings.

Mud or no mud, spring better come soon, Selma thought.

She no more than got Edith and herself dressed and outside when she saw the boys right behind the barn with the cow. "She was good, Mama," they said. "She came right home."

"And you are good, too," she told them. "Bringing in the cows just like a man."

She knew they were a long way from doing a man's work, but they liked to hear it. "Now pick the eggs," she said. "And feed the chickens. And then you can play." She thought they would probably come right in the house to play, as nasty as the day was.

"Henry coming," Christina said, tugging on Selma's coat and pointing out the driveway toward the west.

What is he doing coming from there? Selma thought, looking out where Christina was pointing. *And on horseback?*

She stood out of the wind against the barn wall and waited, but in a few minutes she knew it was not Henry. Another stranger. Three of them in less than a month. She tried not to be afraid, but here she was alone, three children, no help in sight, Henry coming some time today, but not here yet. *There should be a man here for me,* she thought.

Like the deputy and the banker, this man had a tall horse, almost black, and matted with sweat. It had been ridden hard, but now was at a walk to cool out.

And like the deputy and the banker, this man wore a long coat, this one of wool, almost to the ankles as he sat on the horse, and heavy mittens and a felt cap with his ears covered. On his feet were laced felt boots and short rubber overshoes.

Not fancy like the banker, but he does not freeze in that, Selma thought, and she wondered if she was the only one who had ugly horses and poor clothes.

All of this she saw in a moment, then looked at the man himself. He rode...proud, maybe too proud. Up straight...like he was stuck on himself. When he stopped a few feet away he looked down on her for a moment before speaking, another round face and mustache like the banker, but this one not soft, the eyes dark and sharp, the black mustache thick and curving out on the ends like a steer's horns.

He dismounted slowly, turned and extended his hand. "Mrs. Wilbur Metwald?" he said.

"Yes. I am Selma Metwald."

When he spoke it was German, but not all sounding the same as Selma's German. "My name is Otto Wollerman," he said. "I am looking for a housekeeper."

His hand was not so big as that of the banker, but hard and strong, like Selma's hands. He leaned against the horse for a moment, lifting and stretching first one leg and then the other. "I have ridden from Kulm already today," he said. "The knees are telling me about it."

He smiled a little and she was aware again of what she looked like.

"My brother is coming soon to help with the feeding," she said. "Should we go in?"

"Thank you. You have a stall I can put my horse in? Or a blanket for him?"

"No blanket. But...I will harness the team and tie them outside for Henry...my brother. He will need them for feeding the cattle. Your horse can use their stall."

"I will wait," he said.

You could offer to help, Selma thought. But she did not want to say it. He needed a housekeeper. She needed some place to go. She did not want to make him angry the first minute.

Finished with the horses, they walked to the house, Christina holding Selma's hand, the boys already inside. *He says nothing to me,* Selma thought.

And in the house he said nothing either while she got out of her coat, gave the children some bread and told them to stay in their room, poured coffee and brought it to the table.

"I am baking today so there is no fresh bread yet," she said. "I have some *pfefferkuchen* left from Christmas."

"That would be good."

He sat in the chair as he rode the horse. Proud. Stuck on himself. Not a big man, but maybe he wanted to be one. And he did not sweep off his boots.

Selma brought the spicy gingerbread cookies. There were only a dozen left. There should have been many more. The boys must have been into them.

"You have heard of me from the deputy, William Bauman?" Selma asked.

"Yah. Well, more from his wife. She has written to her sister in Kulm telling that a housekeeper is available for someone."

"I would like to thank her some time."

"I am farming north of Edgeley," he said. "But I travel to look at cattle and land, and I came to Kulm. So now I am here."

He dipped a cookie in his coffee and sucked on it before biting.

"The cookies are good."

"Thank you. You have heard what has happened with my husband?"

"Mr. Metwald…yah. I stopped at the saloon for a beer. They talk about him there. Nothing nice." He smiled at her, the ends of his mustache wiggling when he did.

"I am saying nothing nice about him, either," Selma answered. "I have told the children we do not talk about him. But we are living without him. My brother helps so much, but I cannot ask him to do the field work, too. He farms for my mother already. So I must leave here.

I have talked with the bank. When I can travel I must sign papers about the land and cattle, and then work I must find. I am waiting only for better weather to travel with the children."

"I have children, too," he answered. "And my wife, Ruth…she has the consumption."

"I am sorry to hear this."

"She is at home yet," he said, "but maybe will have to go to a sanitarium for some time. Even without that, with the children it is hard for her, and I must do the field work."

"How many children?"

"Two now. Julia is three, my wife's from a first marriage. And little Anna is one, mine with my wife. We will have more I hope."

The both sat silent for a time, sipping the coffee. Selma ate one of the cookies, thinking there might still be some saved for another time, but the man Otto kept at them.

"The house must be kept clean," he said then. "And the meals when my wife cannot work or is gone. And the children need care every day."

"And a garden?"

"Yes, a big garden. She does the gardening, I do the field work."

"So no field work? Animal chores?"

"Only when I am gone. The house and children are enough…and preserving food. You can do that?"

"Yes."

Selma wondered what it was that got people into the situations they were in. All of it from sin? Bad luck? She wanted to talk to someone about her own troubles, even to this man if he would listen, and she wondered if he talked with his wife about their troubles, or if they were sad about the tuberculosis and saying nothing, as Mutter and Vater had done when Vater was sick.

"Your relatives are at Edgeley, too?" Selma asked.

"No. I come to America alone in 1910. From Hammerstein, West Prussia. I am Prussian."

"I do not know about Prussians," Selma said. "My family came from Bessarabia, Russians drove them out. My father is dead, but my mother farms three miles over, and my younger brother with her, and my older brother on the next section…my father was always thinking the old country was better, and he complained about North Dakota…but he was good to the children. No beatings."

She looked to see how this Otto Wollerman would take that. He smiled at her in that stuck-up way. "No beatings in my place either. Children or horses. But a cow is different…"

Selma was surprised to hear her own laughter. It had not happened often this winter. "Yah," she said. "Sometimes a cow makes herself hateful."

"I was a horsetrainer for the Kaiser's armies," he said. "In the 12th Dragoons I served two years. Before that I was in the 141st Infantry one year, and before that on my father's farm working in West Prussia. But I was not satisfied. There is no more land there. So when my enlistment was up I come to America."

"And now there is war in Europe I am told," Selma said. She had only the vaguest idea of Europe and the countries there, but any gossip Henry brought had something about the war. "You are lucky."

"The Germans will win that war," Wollerman said. "Everything is ready for it…the training, the weapons, the railroads, all of it. But I am American now."

"So you do not want to go back for it?"

"No. That war is wrong, and I will have citizenship here. And I am 34 years old."

"With children."

"Yah, with children. And I am a cavalryman but there is no place left for that. The modern weapons are too much, and now I read it will be all trench warfare. Certain death for a cavalryman. But I am sure the generals are still ordering the charges."

"You are lucky to be here."

He sat up straighter. "Not lucky, Mrs. Metwald. I am here by my own decision."

He became more businesslike. Selma thought perhaps she had stepped over a line.

"My house is big," he said. "There will be a room of your own. If you need to see your family I can loan a buggy, or they can come to stay, but only one night. The pay is $15 a month and board."

Selma made a list in her head of things she would need. "Sundays off?" she asked. She had no understanding of how much she should be paid. Fifteen dollars did not sound like much, but she did not want to make him angry by asking for more.

"No, but as little work as possible. We observe the Sabbath as best we can. You go to church?"

"I would like to."

"There is a church two miles from the farm. Lutheran."

"Must I care for your wife when she is weak?"

"Yes, that, too."

"And I need a room for my children."

He hesitated before he answered.

"That is not possible," he said. "Your children cannot come. You must be taking care of my children."

"I cannot go without them," Selma said. "And already the boys become unruly with no father, so I must have a good place for them, and a school."

"I will not allow it," Wollerman said. "Perhaps we cannot make this work."

Christina came to the kitchen asking for a drink of water. She had found her second dress and put it on backward, but shoes she could not manage yet. Selma was glad the floors were clean so the child's stockings would not look grubby.

Wollerman looked at the child a moment, then asked, "What is your name, little girl?"

"Stina," she answered promptly. "Stina, Stina, Stina, Stina."

He laughed. "Can you come here, little Stina?"

She walked close to him, but not close enough he could pick her up. She pointed at his face, then put her finger on her own face just below her nose where a mustache might grow.

"Schnauze's tail," she said.

Selma blushed. "Sh-h-h," she said. "Don't you say that."

Wollerman laughed and laughed.

"Go and play," Selma said, and Christina went back to her brothers.

"Schnauze is the black horse," Selma said, and then thought that didn't make it any better.

"Then this is the first time a child calls me a horse's behind," Wollerman said.

Selma blushed again. "I am sorry for her. She speaks what she wants to."

"Would your family keep your children?" Wollerman asked. "Perhaps it would be temporary."

"I cannot bring them?"

"Not at first for certain. There is too much to do with my family."

Up and down things go, Selma thought. *Nowhere to go, then this man has work, so somewhere to go, but now he makes it so difficult, so...*

But she had no other choices.

"If I leave my boys, $20 a month," she said. "I would have to send money for them."

"That is very high for a housekeeper. Fifteen was generous."

"Twenty dollars and I must have Christina with me."

He thought about it for a moment and then again came that stuck-up smile under the big mustache.

"We can try it then," he said.

Selma thought about the bread she had rising and jumped up. The loaf nearest the heat was going to be too big and fluffy, so she set it aside and put the rest in the oven.

"There will not be room for your furniture," Wollerman said. "You can bring only enough for your room."

"*Es macht nicht*, it makes no difference," Selma answered. "I have very little. Some lamps perhaps, and a bedside table, a chest of drawers?"

"Yah. Whatever we can take in a buckboard. As soon as the roads are open I will come for you. The fifteenth of May?"

Selma watched through the window as Wollerman brought his horse from the barn, tightened the cinch, and mounted. He had to give a jump to reach the stirrup, but he made it look easy.

After a few steps Wollerman set the horse into the same long trot the other visitors had used with their driving horses. He rose slightly in his stirrups with alternate strides, and in minutes he was out the rutted lane and onto the road. A quick flurry of snow blew by and she saw him no more.

That must be how a cavalryman rides a horse, Selma thought. *And that is how a Prussian talks.*

So now the future was not so cloudy. She would move north of Edgeley, a town just as far from Kulm as where Selma lived, but east, not south. She would do housework for a Prussian cavalryman farmer who had two children, maybe more, and a wife with the tuberculosis. She would not have to feed cattle and hogs, would not have to pitch hay and wrestle sacks of grain. She would have room and board and $20 a month, and something in savings if the banker was honest with what he had told her, and there would be no beatings.

That alone is something different, she thought, though she had heard stories of husbands far worse than Wilbur Metwald had been.

And for the time being she must leave the boys...if Mutter and Henry agreed. She hoped they would, but she already felt guilty that she must ask, guilty that she must leave Rudy and Daniel. What kind of a mother would leave her children? But perhaps that kind was better than a mother who let her children starve, or one who let their father beat them. And Wollerman had said it might only be temporary.

Leaving them was not the same as what Wilbur had done. *Not the same at all,* she said to herself repeatedly.

She wondered what Mrs. Wollerman was like. Anyone with serious sickness could be difficult. She knew that from what Vater had been like.

Still, maybe there would be good days, days when the two of them could visit. Or maybe the woman would be stuck-up like the man. But maybe someone in the church would be good to visit.

So. A stuck-up Prussian cavalryman farmer with a big mustache. One who seemed to like children, even if they called him a horse's behind.

That Christina. What a child to say things.

Selma caught herself laughing for the second time today. *March has been better than November was,* she told herself.

She was anxious to tell Henry.

Chapter Four

Autumn 1916

Julia was soon five, a strong, blue-eyed, quiet child who watched everything but stood aside from it. Mrs. Wollerman, Ruth, had said from the beginning that Julia would not have to be doing chores in the house until she was ready for it, and Mr. Wollerman didn't give the child any work either. *So in the house is a pair of eyes without hands,* Selma thought. There were things the child should be doing more than playing with her rag doll and watching the grown-ups.

Two-year-old Anna had been put to bed for the night and their mother had gone to her own room, too. Selma would bring Ruth a little warm milk with cinnamon and sugar in it after a while and ask if there was any more to do. In the meantime, there were hog intestines that needed scraping and washing, and Julia could be learning to do it instead of just watching.

"I am helping, Mama," Christina kept saying, and she would scrape a bit of fat from the tough, slimy tube, which Selma was turning inside out. But it would only be for a minute, and some of that not getting it clean, and then she would wander off.

Christina was four, not much younger than Julia, so maybe it was too much to expect from Julia, too. *Maybe tonight I am just tired of*

73

having children underfoot, Selma thought.

She decided she could get more done if she put Julia and Christina to bed. At least one long string of the intestines had to be done tonight. Tomorrow would be frying meatballs to pack in lard for cold storage, trimming the flank slabs for bacon, sawing up the ribs for soup bones, boiling the brains for head cheese, grinding the loose pieces with spices, and stuffing short pieces of intestine with that mixture for smoked sausages.

"Everything is used but the squeal," everyone said about hogs.

"And that is saved for wives to call husbands from the field," was the rest of the saying.

The good thing was that all three girls got along together. At first Selma had worried that Julia would pick on Christina from jealousy, but that had not happened, and she had worried that Christina would pick on little Anna just because that is the way with children when they see their mother giving attention to another. But that had not happened either.

Selma had to be careful to give Julia and Anna as much attention as she gave Christina, that much she had been told by Mrs. Wollerman, but all of the children were expected to entertain themselves, and as long as they were together they were good to do that except in the evening when they were tired.

Not so much fighting with them as with Rudy and Daniel, but it was not right that the boys were still not allowed to join her. She had not seen them since summer for part of two days when her mother had come with them to the Wollerman farm, and that during haying when there was a crew to cook for. And she would not see them again until Christmas when she would travel to the Retzlaff farm herself if the weather was good.

But it could not be helped.

Julia and Anna slept together in a full-sized bed, which they had to give up if there was company. Selma tucked them in and sat with them for a while.

"Time to sleep now," Selma told them.

Christina slept with Selma in another full-sized bed. The room was small, just enough for the bed, a wash-stand, a chest of drawers with a mirror, and one chair. But it was enough. Selma would sometimes read a bit of the Bible late at night by the light of a lamp, but other than that and sleeping she was not much in the room. A small grate in the floor brought up heat from the kitchen. The room still was cold on the worst nights, but not once had she had ice on the chamber pot.

Once she was alone again in the kitchen she worked quickly, pulling the intestine out of a five-gallon porcelain crock on her left, turning it inside-out a foot or so at a time, scraping it clean against the board set between the two crocks, brushing the fatty leavings off the board into a bucket in the center, dropping the cleaned intestines into the crock on her right.

Mrs. Wollerman had only been gone to the sanatarium once, for a couple of months. Selma had missed her for that time, missed the help, but most of all missed the company. Ruth did not do much work. She was not strong, and if she worked hard enough to speed up her breathing then the coughing would start. That would put her back in her room for hours, since she did not want anyone to have to listen, and she did not want anyone to see the bloody phlegm coming with it.

They were not such friends that Selma should forget being a hired woman. But at least there was a grown-up to visit with. They talked about the war, what little they knew. They talked about what the children were doing. They tried to teach the children their ABCs and to count and to know their colors. They figured out what needed sewing, what the pantry needed, what the garden was doing, how to get food out to Otto and any hired men in the fields, what to buy in Edgeley, what to cook for celebrations at the church.

Ruth would do the dishes and pretend to teach Julia that job. Some days she would clear the table. Some Sundays she felt well enough to dress her own girls for going to church, and in church it was Ruth who kept the girls from becoming restless.

Selma looked forward to those Sundays because if Ruth felt that good, Selma could stay after church and visit with other women. Most were wives who went on home when the husbands did, but some were the other way, wives who liked to stay and talk, with husbands who didn't hurry them.

Ruth did almost all the talking with Mr. Wollerman. Selma was glad for that. The man was good enough to her, Selma, never complaining about her work, sometimes playing a minute with Christina. But most of the time he said nothing to her or Christina. He joked with the other two girls and talked childish with them. When Ruth had been gone it had been the same except to tell Selma, "Do this, do that," once in a while. She had been happy to see Ruth come home.

But it was a good household. Otto—Mr. Wollerman—worked as hard as any man Selma had ever seen, as hard as Vater or her brothers ever did. And he was smart about it, she could tell from what he told Ruth. Always thinking how to get the most work done quickest, always looking for something to read about the crops or the animals, always talking about how to get cows that gave more milk, beef cattle that grew quicker, horses that were the strongest and quietest, animal medicines that worked better and cheaper.

"When the creamery is going in Edgeley we will have money coming in every month," he told Ruth more than once at the supper table. "Milking more cows is more work, and a hired man we will need all the time. But it will pay. It will pay."

"More money and you will just buy another horse," Ruth would tease him. "Or drink more beer."

He would laugh at her when she said that. "No, I would only have enough to buy more pretty dresses for my wife and girls," he would answer. "Nothing is ever left for poor Papa."

In time Selma had learned that he, Mr. Wollerman, was the center of the family, the center of the whole farm.

Wilbur Metwald had been the center of their farm. Selma was not surprised that Wollerman would be the same. The difference was that Wollerman was good to his family, good to his animals, working day and night to be a good farmer, except when he drank too much beer and became like any other man with that.

So that stuck-up look of his is more from what he makes of himself than from thinking he is better than others, Selma thought, scraping and scraping. *He is proud of what he is doing.* But the Bible said something about pride going before the fall. She hoped she wouldn't be around when it happened.

While Mr. Wollerman was the center of what the family was doing, it was Ruth's illness that was the center of what the family was thinking.

"Ruth's illness..." Otto began much of his talk when there was company.

"Mama's sickness..." came from Julia and Anna.

The adults talked about it at times, Ruth even confiding in Selma that she hoped if the end did come it would happen quickly rather than with the long times of coughing and choking she had seen with others. But as soon as she said that, she would change her talking to how she had to get better for the children.

"Children should never be without a mother," she would say. "And I cannot bear to think of being without them."

She doesn't think what that means to me, Selma thought each time.

So in the house were five bedrooms, the one downstairs with Otto and Ruth, and upstairs Selma and Christina in one, Julia and Anna in one, the smallest room waiting for a new baby, and the last, the biggest room, Ruth's mother, Frederika Schloven, who came from Edgeley to help when Ruth needed, or when Ruth was gone.

And if I had been told of her I would have been more worried to come here, Selma often thought.

Mrs. Schloven seemed to be everything gray—her hair of course, but her clothing, even her way of moving and talking, always slow and quiet, never happy but not so sad others could feel sorry for her, never complaining but not quite satisfied with what Selma got done. At least that was how Selma worried about her. She did not visit with Selma as Ruth would, and Selma thought maybe it was not something with Selma Metwald, but something about a single woman in Ruth's house.

Selma was finishing the scraping when she heard the slow steps of Mrs. Schloven coming down the stairs and toward the kitchen. She had never raised her voice to Selma, yet those footsteps made Selma anxious, because always something might be said.

"My glass was empty," she said now, the glass in her hand.

"I am sorry," Selma answered. "I will fill it and bring it up to you."

"I will get it," Mrs. Schloven said. She looked at what Selma was doing. "We will need more sausage skins tomorrow," she said.

"This much is ready," Selma said, looking at the crock nearly full.

"More than that," Mrs. Schloven told her.

Selma knew what it meant. Do another one, tonight, even though Mrs. Schloven and no one else, either, could guess just how much was needed.

Then she felt a little guilty. The woman had not said that, after all. Maybe it was just talk.

She warmed a bit of milk and took it to Ruth who was sitting in her rocking chair by the bed, still dressed, her hair let down, a book by the lamp. "Thank you, Selma," she said. "It was a good day. We got many things done. And the coughing did not come at all."

"Yah, and tomorrow will be good, too," Selma answered.

Ruth was always kind that way.

In the kitchen Selma set out slices of a cold ham, some cheese and dill pickles, some white bread and the butter dish, and some bean soup she had kept warm. Mr. Wollerman came in from the barn, leaving his boots and coat in the porch but still bringing the barn stink with him. He washed his hands at the sink and went at the food hungrily.

"Even with pig guts in the kitchen I am hungry tonight," he said.

"I am sorry for that," Selma answered. She was starting on a second crock. "The children were taking my time today and this did not get done."

"My day was like that," he said. "So much time butchering I did not get the feeding done until now."

He watched her quick hands for a minute. "I think one would be enough for tomorrow," he said then.

"Mrs. Schloven thinks we will need more."

She heard him say something like, "Hunh."

Selma wanted to quit and go to her room, but she thought about how it would be the next day if they should have to stop what they were doing and wait while she cleaned another string of intestines.

"I will finish this second one," she said to Wollerman. "So I will not

78

have to do it tomorrow."

He seemed to have lost interest, finishing his supper quickly. "Ruth is feeling good tonight?" he asked then.

"Yes, I think so. She has had no coughing for two days."

"Good night, then."

"Good night."

Selma scraped and scraped, her hands and wrists tired but in her mind thinking how her life was, and how it had been with Wilbur, and wondering if this was the rest of it or if she was waiting again for something. And she thought again of her boys and how it must be for Mutter and Henry to be raising them, and Mutter not so young...63 this year. And she thought of what she would do and where she would go when Ruth died, and that would come, even if Ruth and Otto didn't think so, because Selma had heard the coughing when it was bad, and she had seen the bloody phlegm, and she did not think miracles happened when the consumption was that far along.

It is a good household, a good family, she thought. She set the crocks on the porch, scrubbed up the scraping board, set the pail of scrapings outside until morning. There was much here that could go wrong—Ruth's illness, Ruth's pregnancy, all the dangers of a farm, all the sicknesses of children—but until that, a good house, and something of a life for her, Selma, though it could not go on forever. That she knew, and what would come after it she did not.

She started for her room, pausing in the front room to hold up the lamp so she could look at the photograph of Otto. It was oval, nearly two feet across, an ornately-carved frame around it, hand-tinted in soft colors so she could see that his uniform coat had been green, his trousers white, his leather knee-boots glistening. He was mounted on a sleek and powerful black horse, its legs caught in mid-stride, its head raised, neck arched, chin tucked in by a polished brass bit hanging from a black bridle. From the saddle Otto stared out at the world. Behind the man on his horse was a park or parade ground with men in suits watching the horse and rider.

He says he is something, Selma thought each time she looked at it. Not a farmer.

A cavalryman. A Prussian. A man who had been to school, a man who did not need to hurt with fists or words those who were weaker, yet a man who scorned weakness in other men. Not a man like Wilbur Metwald, but a man who would do what he said he would do.

She had seen all that in him, yet seen, too, that he sometimes was not everything he thought of himself. She thought Ruth must understand that, and that he must understand that he did not fool Ruth, because the two of them were, like Mutter and Vater had once been, such good friends. It was plain that they enjoyed talking to each other, were proud to be seen with each other, even though the illnesses, the work, the bank, the weather, the crops, the animals, were always something in the way.

Selma went up the stairs quietly, the lamp throwing moving shadows on the walls.

Maybe that is what I am waiting for yet, she thought. Like a fifteen-year-old girl.

And I will be waiting for it when I die, she thought. *It is not for everyone. That I have learned.*

Christmas 1917

All of December Selma worked to prepare the house for Christmas. She would be gone herself, and Ruth could not do all the cooking and cleaning that were necessary. Selma did not even get to church on Sundays, instead cooking ahead some more so that all Ruth and Mrs. Schloven would need is to warm up the meals.

It was the second Christmas Selma had been allowed to travel to her mother's farm. She was grateful for the chance, though the trip was difficult—two days each way with horse and cutter, just Selma and Christina and the cold winds and snowdrifts and the road not always visible.

It could have been done in one day if she had wanted to travel cross-country and use the horse harder, but she was afraid to lose her way, and Mr. Wollerman did not want his horse hurt. So she stayed with the main county road, through Edgeley and on to Kulm one day and out to the Retzlaff farm the next.

She mentioned to no one that in Edgeley she had her photograph taken in a good black dress and hat. She did not know why she wanted it, but she had been thinking of it for a long time.

She could see at the Retzlaff place that things could not always be the same there. Mutter was now 64, Rudy 11, Daniel 9. Both boys were helping on at the place, but both still were not minding Mutter very well.

"They are good boys," Mutter kept saying, "but they are boys. I cannot keep up with them, and Henry does not think he should be the one telling them things."

Mutter had become heavy and slow, though she still worked ceaselessly. Her hands were big for a woman, powerful, but knotting up with arthritis. Sometimes she sat holding her hands over the stove, rubbing the joints of one hand between the thumb and fingers of the other. She had no teeth left, and she kept her lips together, moving them limply in rhythm with her hands.

Still she insisted they cook and cook, so it would be Christmas. Three days in the kitchen was preparing for Christmas dinner when Emelia and Martin would come with their children, Ludwig and Eva with theirs, Henry still alone living with Mutter.

Mutter had made sauerkraut of course, earlier in the fall, so it was ready to heat with sausages, and she had pickled a few watermelons. But now was time for baking *pfeffernuse*, not only because they were traditional and tasty, but because they would keep for months. And Mutter wanted *portzilke*, the deep-fired batter cakes for New Year.

"They are for taking to the neighbors," Selma reminded her. "And you will not be traveling anywhere at New Year."

"But still," Mutter chuckled. "New Year will come, and what is New Year without *portzilke*."

And, of course, there were strudels to make. Selma was the best at that now, her fingers swift and nimble, thinning the dough as it laid in round sheets across her arm. "Vater would like to see you doing that," Mutter said.

"I don't think he was much for watching it," Selma smiled. "More for eating."

"Like Rudy and Daniel," Mutter said. "Always eating."

And now comes the question, Selma thought.

"Will the boys come to live with you soon?" Mutter asked.

"I hope so. It is too long now. But the mister does not say it yet. The house is full and a baby coming soon. It would be difficult."

"And the Mrs. Wollerman?"

"She is getting weaker, I think. And having a baby coming is so hard for her. And the mister…he knows. It will be terrible for everyone if she dies. Mrs. Schloven helps, but I do not know what she would do if Ruth was gone. So the troubles are there, and they all know, but still they talk about life more than about…"

Mutter was rubbing her hands again at the stove. "They talk with you about these things?" she asked.

"No. Well, Mrs. Wollerman a little. But they talk to each other, and they don't care if I hear. They…they are always talking together…like you and Vater did."

She looked at Mutter and saw the fleshy chin begin to quiver, the eyes to water up. When Mutter spoke, her voice was catching. "So many years," she said. "The farm changes, my body changes…" she smiled at that, "…and not to be better. And the family changes, but the feelings stay the same."

"I miss him still," Selma said.

"Yah. And me, of course. But I feel bad for you, too, because you never…"

"When I was fifteen I thought I was waiting for a life like you and Vater had. Then I thought it would come with Wilbur Metwald."

Mutter shook her head. Her chin was still quivering and she dabbed at her eyes with a handkerchief. "I have so much wished for you…"

"It does not happen to everyone," Selma said. "Not to many. So…" She shrugged her shoulders. "Still, I must live and work, and Christina is a good child. But I wish the boys could come with me."

When the boys did come to the kitchen she wanted to hold them, but they stood off from her. Rudy was already almost as tall as Selma. Both boys were lean and strong and quick moving, like Wilbur, Selma thought, and looking around for something for themselves more than looking at the other person.

Like Wilbur that way, too. But what could be expected, being raised the way it was turning out, and them knowing their father had deserted them?

"Are the cookies done?" Daniel asked.

Selma gave them four each, plain sugar cookies, still warm. They took the cookies and went back outside.

"So much you give them," Mutter said.

"Not so much if I see them only once or twice a year. They are not bothering the teacher, I hope," Selma said. "I am sure they do not like sitting in a desk."

"The teacher is rough," Mutter said. "She will hit them any time they do wrong. Daniel is not afraid of her, but Rudy is. So they are learning still, but I think Rudy will not last much longer there."

"I hope they can get more schooling," Selma said. "The Mr. Wollerman has been eight years before he came to America, and it helps him with the farming. He is reading always about how to farm better, and about the war and the government."

"Maybe they will stay in it," Mutter replied. "There is a new teacher almost every year. If they like the teacher it helps. And if I had a pony to pull a cart or cutter for them it would help, but I will not let them use a big horse. So they walk, and they don't like that. Some days I think they walk until I cannot see them, then just play in the fields instead of going to school."

Selma took trays of cookies to the porch to cool. "No more now," she called out to the boys. She had to set the trays up on a shelf because the screen door was ripped and the dog went in and out of the porch by himself.

That isn't the only thing that needs fixing in this house, Selma thought. The windows were filthy. The linoleum that Mutter had once been so proud of for the kitchen floor, so carefully hauled from town when it came, was the same as when Selma had lived at home, and it was worn through to the bare boards at the sink and the cooking counter. Mutter did not seem to care, and Henry was a bachelor. A man didn't look.

This life here, like my life at the Wollerman farm, cannot go on much longer the way it has been, Selma thought again.

She still thought of the house as new, and it had been new when she was a child, but that was already many years.

"Mr. Wollerman is not harsh with you?" Mutter asked when Selma returned to the kitchen.

"No. We do not speak much, but he is good."

"And he does not...look at you? Touch you?"

"What are you asking? You think he might think of me in that way?"

"He is a man. I have seen him."

"I think he is a man so worried about his wife that he has nothing else on his mind."

Mutter shook her head. "I feel sorry for them," she said. "Still, if the missus is gone, that will change."

"When the missus dies I will have to leave there."

Mutter shook her head again. "Yes, but he may ask you to stay. He will still need someone for the house, and for Julia and Anna. Who else would he have now? And if that happens...you will be..."

"I would have to leave, Mutter. As I said."

"It will not be as easy as that."

"What are you saying?"

"If he is a decent man..."

"That he is."

"...then he will be heartbroken. He will want...comforting."

"I cannot give that. It would not be right, and he will not look for comfort from me. I am the hired woman. That is all. He makes nothing else of it...and if you mean he will need someone in his bed..."

"He is a man."

"And I am Selma Metwald still. Alone. But not divorced. I would like to be, but I am not divorced, and I am not a loose woman. So I don't think this is something we talk about anymore."

And they did not. But at night Selma thought about it, and she wondered.

The second day was more cooking, but in the afternoon Selma hitched up the Wollerman horse and took her three children for a ride in the cutter, urging the horse along as fast as he would trot across the fields, first to Ludwig and Eva's farm, then to Emily and Martin's. They had to skirt long narrow rows of trees, mixed growths of spruce, elms, ash, poplars, and Russian olive, windbreaks that had been planted when Selma was a child and which now were grown tall.

The boys had a pair of wooden skis held on with leather straps and took turns being pulled on a rope behind the cutter. "Faster, faster!" they shouted at Selma, but she would not let the horse break into a gallop. Even at the trot they sometimes tumbled, especially if she went up and over a few small drifts close together, and she would stop to help them brush off the snow and get ready to go again.

"Just go," they told her, but she insisted they get rid of the snow first.

"You must not get wet," she said. "You will freeze if you get wet."

A mother must teach her children these things.

She did not know what Mr. Wollerman would say if he saw her working the horse this hard for fun. But the children needed something besides school and work and old people.

They only stayed a few minutes at each stop, enough to let the horse catch his wind and cool down. Rudy and Daniel were familiar with Ludwig's children and with Emily's, some younger, some older. But Christina was shy with them and she did not yet understand what was a cousin, though she knew she had seen them other times.

"Remember their names," Selma told her. "They come to Grandma's house on Christmas like last year."

On the way home she let the boys ski some more, but with a half-mile to go she slowed the horse to a walk. The boys sat in the cutter with her, not room for four, but they all huddled under the blankets anyway, Christina on Rudy's lap. Selma wanted to hold them all in her arms, but she needed both hands for the driving lines.

On Christmas Day the house was so full there was no room even to sit except on the floor. Children ran everywhere, playing, then arguing, then crying, then playing again, dropping piles of outdoor clothes when they came inside all sweaty, digging in those piles to get dressed for going back out.

Emily had four, almost five, from thirteen years down to three. "And this next one any day now," she said, her hands on her enormous stomach. "I am so glad you came to help Mutter make Christmas. I cannot move much more than to get myself dressed."

Ludwig and Eva had six boys the same ages as Emily and Martin's.

"Maybe we get a girl next time," Eva always said.

Ludwig himself was black-haired and lean, strong as he had been when he helped Selma dig Vater's grave. When he wasn't farming he was blacksmithing, and the extra money meant he was getting ahead on his place.

It was Emily who spoke about Henry. "He is courting Martin's sister," she told Selma. It was the first Selma had heard.

"If they marry maybe he will have this farm for his own," Selma said.

"We must talk about that, you and me and Ludwig and Henry," Emily answered.

"Henry should have his own," Selma went on. "He has worked so hard for Mutter, and for me."

"And sometimes for Ludwig," Emily said. She shuffled about the kitchen, her face heavy like her body. "Ahh," she said. "Sitting hurts, laying down hurts, standing hurts, moving around is too hard, and the baby kicks me black and blue."

She laughed then. "If this one is early and makes another Christmas present, I would be happy for that."

She walked about some more in small circles. "I think Henry sees that Ludwig is getting ahead. Martin and I are buying more land, and if the crops are good again, this year an automobile. Ludwig is doing better yet. For Henry there would be the home quarter and the quarter Mutter homesteaded, but both need much more work. Fences are bad, weeds, new outbuildings will be needed. Mutter has not made anything new. Henry could break himself working and still not keep up with his older brother and sister. At least that is what I think. I hope that does not turn him away."

"The four of us need to talk about this," Selma said.

"Yah, this afternoon when the dinner is done."

And talk they did, sitting in the front room, Mutter having gone to take a little nap, the children thumping around upstairs. As long as there was no screaming or crying, and as long as it wasn't too quiet, the grown-ups didn't interfere.

What to do with Mutter when she could no longer work the place, that they asked each other over and over. And it would be soon. Another year, maybe two.

"If Henry gets married he should have some time without caring for her," Eva said. "He has done his share already here." Ludwig nodded his agreement, and Selma could see that this was right.

"Emma, she wants only to stay near where there is family," Martin Seibern said. "If she has to help with your mother she will…I think. She has not said no. But she does not tell me everything either. I am the older brother, so that means I am not so smart as she is…"

"Yah, that is what I think of Ludwig," Selma teased, and they all laughed at that, but Ludwig not as much.

"I don't think Mutter would be happy to leave the place, only if it is for me and Emma to be newlyweds," Henry said. "It would not be right to move her that way."

"If you take over the farm you should not have all the cost of keeping Mutter, even if she lives here," Emily said to Henry.

"But he would get the land," Ludwig said. "For that he should expect some costs."

Henry did not argue with that, so they agreed on it, and then Ludwig asked what to do with Mutter's homestead quarter.

"Rent it out if the family cannot farm it," Emily answered. "But first it should stay in the family if any of us can farm it, or part of it."

"I don't want any more rent land, Emily," Martin told her. "I will buy more, but not that piece. So if Henry and Ludwig can work something out…but if there is some rent from it that would be a pension for your mother."

"Well, I would keep on farming some of it," Henry said. "And if Ludwig wants to rent part, then it would get better care. It is too much for me to to all of it with the home place."

Emily looked around at all of them. "When Mutter dies," she said, "that homestead quarter should go to Selma. She needs it most."

"And you get nothing?" Selma asked. "That is not right."

"Martin and I are doing fine without it," Emily answered.

"It is too soon to decide that," Ludwig said then. "Mutter is not failing yet. She is just not able to work like when she was young. So, we wait with that."

For the first time Selma thought of Ludwig as something more than her older brother. *He is becoming a judge for the family*, she thought. She did not know if it was good, but she did not feel as if she could argue with him.

"And where will Mutter go when she needs help living?" Eva asked. "Our house is full with children, but after a few more years…"

"She can stay here still," Henry said.

"The stairs are too much if she gets weak," Selma told him. "And I think that would be too much for you and Emma if you have already kept her some years."

"We have the summer kitchen yet," Ludwig said. "With some better windows and doors and a coal stove I can make it work for her for winter. But if the arthritis gets bad and she cannot walk, then it would be too much for Eva…"

"I still hope to have a baby girl some day," Eva said, and she blushed as she looked at Ludwig. "And I am expecting again for this summer…"

"Then when the time comes I will take her," Selma told them. The conversation was becoming strange, as if they were deciding someone's life for that person. She hoped they were doing the right thing.

"What would you do with her?" Emily asked Selma. "You have no place."

"The time will come when I must leave the Wollerman place," Selma replied. "I will need to find something else then, and I would try to find something where Mutter could be with me."

"Well, if that happens, fine and good," Ludwig said. "But in the meantime, she lives here if Henry and Emma agree, then our summer kitchen, and after that whatever Emily can do, and after that, Selma. And Mutter's homestead quarter…I think we wait until Mutter cannot care for herself, and then deed it to whomever has her."

So it was settled, and it was another moment when Selma thought time was beyond understanding. It seemed so long ago, yet it seemed just yesterday, that the place had been new, that Vater had been sitting in this same house complaining about the Russians, that the family had been new in North Dakota. She could even remember vaguely a few moments from the sod house, that time the horse stepped through the roof, and the first she knew of it Emily shrieking. *And here we sit,* she thought, *this new house showing its age, this farm falling behind while other farms are growing, each of us with another life not of this here, and our own children already the ages we were then.*

In that time Vater was gone, and Martha, and Ludwig and Eva's stillborn child.

And tomorrow I go back to a house where more are leaving soon, she thought.

She had that thought again early in the morning, dressing Christina for the cold journey, saying good-bye to Mutter, holding the boys as long as she could make them stand for it.

"I hope soon you can come to live with me," she said tearfully.

"With Grandma and Uncle Henry is good enough," Daniel replied, and that made it worse, but she did not scold him for it.

Once the Wollerman horse left the driveway and turned north it was the right direction for him, and he stayed at his work so steadily Selma had trouble slowing him to a walk occasionally so he wouldn't be worn out.

Returning to a house where more would be leaving soon made her sad. And what if Mr. Wollerman…what if he had thoughts as Mutter had said. That made her worried, but she also worried that now it had been said out loud, she was having thoughts about him, too. *And what does God think of that?* she asked herself.

It was better not to think about it, better not to have heard it said at all.

Yet she was anxious to get back. It was where her life was now, even if it was a life more for others than for herself.

A tiny woman and her bundled-up daughter, she traveled from one house where a life was fading, to another the same, the gliding cutter rocking them gently, here and there a hawk hunting low, only twice that first day another traveler on the vast, silent landscape.

October 1918

In the late evening Selma was darning socks, sitting in the front room with a lamp, waiting for Otto Wollerman to come in. Each day he was plowing stubble until dark and then coming home to milk two cows and do the chores. A hired man was plowing, too, with his own four horses, but he worked them only five or six hours and then had to travel home four miles. Otto was using up two hitches of four horses each day, one hitch for the morning and early afternoon, the other for afternoon and evening. The weather was good, frost at night but warm, sunny days, mild wind and no rain. He said he was anxious to get the plowing finished.

Nice out, Selma thought. No bugs, not too hot, not too cold. She had carried lunches to the field with Anna at noon. Late robins had been picking at worms in the soft dirt turned up by the plowshares. Both men had been at the far end of the field and not yet turned around, and Selma knew that even before they started back, Otto would rest the horses, lift the collars to cool their necks, look them over for places the harnesses might rub a sore.

She thought it was like the time he came to offer her the housekeeping work. The horse must work hard and behave, but for that it gets good care.

So Selma and Anna had left the lunches and walked back to the house, taking their time. Two flocks of geese they saw high up. *They are plowing, too,* Selma thought. *Plowing for the South because they know the good weather cannot last.* The day before she had seen a flock of white swans doing the same, and after them hundreds of gray sandhill cranes whooping and calling, and everywhere on the ground blackbirds by the thousands, whirling away with red flashing from their wings.

Nice out, but in a couple of months Christmas already, and by then nice weather would only be a memory.

And she thought this would not be a happy Christmas.

In the one week Selma had been gone over the last Christmas, the Wollerman house had not seemed to change, but by the end of January Selma had seen it was changing quickly for the worse. And now, in October, she knew that even after all the changes of the year, another must happen, because she was no longer just waiting in the evening for Otto to come in so she could finish her work. She was waiting for his conversation, his company, for Otto himself. She had let herself say it, even if it meant she was thinking again like when she was fifteen years old.

In January Ruth's baby had come. Mr. Wollerman had gone for a mid-wife to stay in the house soon after Selma had returned. "A doctor would be better, and if we can get one we will," he said to Selma. "But if there is not time for that I want someone here. Mrs. Schloven cannot always be here, and you have with the children enough work."

"I am grateful for that," she had told him. "Even with three births of my own I have no experience with the mid-wifing."

Ruth's last days before the birth had been difficult. *She is like my sister Emily suffering,* Selma had thought, *but not healthy like Emily.* Any kind of moving around brought on the coughing, and that was too dangerous, so Ruth was almost bedridden, and when the baby came it was all one night and part of the next day.

Otto brought a doctor from Edgeley in the night, and with the doctor and the mid-wife the baby was born and Ruth was as good as could be expected. Through it Otto had been outside only for the least chores. The rest of the time he sat at the kitchen table, and whatever was in his head came out in words to Selma, and she knew that was another quick change in the house. After it she could look back to that time as an ending and the beginning.

"I have a son," he had told her at noon on the birth day, his face beaming. "We name him August, a name from my mother. And Ruth is well…and I have plans for August. By the time he is grown I will own land instead of renting, and we will have a tractor, and we will farm it together as I did with my father, and there is no troubles like in Prussia so he can stay on the place, and plenty more land to buy if we need, so

91

he will not get pushed aside."

It was the first time Selma heard a hint of what had brought the man to America. But by afternoon of that same day he had not been so happy. "Little August is weak," he told her, although she already knew. She had been in and out of the room for the bedpans and clean sheets and bringing wash water.

He sat again at the table, his head in his hands. "I must pray for him," he said. "But I have for a long time not been in prayer. Not since…not since I was a child. August does not breathe right, the doctor says. His crying is not strong. I should pray…"

Selma felt sorry for him, but she did not know what to say so she was glad she did not have time to talk. She kept out bread and butter, liverwurst, and potato soup for everyone.

In the late afternoon Ruth's parents came in a sleigh. Mr. Schloven left immediately but Mrs. Schloven stayed, so Selma was able to take the girls outside for a while, away from the worry in the house. She pulled them on a sled along the driveway and around the outbuildings.

"You girls have been good," she told them. "So quiet. Maybe tomorrow you can play more."

"Mama was shouting," Anna said. "I heard her. She is angry at the new baby?"

"No, she is not angry," Selma answered. "When the baby comes it hurts Mama a little, and that is why the shouting."

"Where does the baby come from?" Christina asked. Selma knew the question would happen.

"From Mama's big stomach," Julia answered. "He is tiny and he was in there."

"I could hold him like my dolly," Anna said. "Pull faster, Selma."

"Why is Papa praying?" Julia asked.

She sees everything, Selma thought before she answered. "He is happy for having a baby boy, I think. So he thanks God." A little lie. It could not be helped.

"The baby is sick," Julia told Anna. "The doctor tells Papa. Selma, is the baby going to die?"

"No, the baby will not die. He will become strong, but it takes a while. You will see. In the summer you will be playing with him, pulling him around in a wagon."

"I think he is going to die," Julia said. "The doctor says he is not breathing right."

"Look," Selma told them. "There are three jackrabbits by the granary. Should we chase them?"

"Yah, yah, chase the rabbits," Christina shouted.

She could only run a little pulling the sled, but the girls thought it was fun. No more questions about the baby for a minute.

Late that evening, the girls in bed for the night, Mrs. Schloven in her own room, the mid-wife sitting with Ruth and the doctor gone back to Edgeley, Selma had returned to the kitchen to do the dishes and put away the food. Otto had still been at the table.

"I have been sitting with Ruth for a while," he said. "She is so pale, and now coughing and the bleeding starts again, so she asks me to go out for while."

"She is always thinking of others," Selma said, and without thinking she had sat across the table from him. "I have been happy here because of that. She does not treat me like a hired girl."

She thought she should not have said that, because Mr. Wollerman did treat her like a hired girl, so now what would he think.

But he had not said anything to that. "The doctor says she may have to go to the sanitarium when she can travel," he said instead. "But first she must nurse little August until he is stronger. Then you will be caring for him, too, until she gets back. I was so happy for a son, and now it gets to be complicated."

The kerosene lamp had not been turned up. It sat on the stove shelf across the room, leaving the table almost in the dark. Selma listened to his voice and saw that she was looking at him, and he at her.

"What will you do if she does not come home?" she asked. "That is a hard question, and I am sorry, but I think it must be said."

She had never seen a man crying, and this one she would not either, but his chin was quivering like Mutter's had been a few days past.

"Yah, it needs to be said. And I do not have an answer. I must farm, and my girls and August must be cared for. There is no one I can send them to except the Schlovens, and they are not young. That is where it all starts."

He looked at her silently until he had himself controlled. "And for you?" he had asked then.

"I cannot go back to my family. Too much is settled there that I would be in the way. So I must work somewhere else."

She took a deep breath. Perhaps it was wrong to say it when he was weak, but she thought, *We are talking now, so perhaps say everything.*

"I must have my boys with me. That I know. And your girls are like my Christina to me. That I know. And August…he must have someone. But my boys need their mother. It is bad enough that their father left them, but it is too much not to have a mother. Their uncle does not teach them like they need because it is not his to do. And my mother is getting slower."

She had an idea that might make it sound better.

"But they are old enough to be helping here if…if I was telling them and they had a man teaching them," she said.

For a minute he had said nothing and Selma had been thinking he doesn't know I am here. Then he had told her. "I have been thinking about them. I know it is not good for you the way it is. But all of it together is too much right now. We must do one thing at a time, maybe until summer. Then…ask again."

It was all they had said at the time, but afterward Selma thought of it as an agreement, the first of many between them, the first of many times they talked across the table in a dimly-lit kitchen.

But nothing this year becomes less complicated, she thought, finishing one sock and starting on another. She caught herself rocking as she worked, and she wondered, *Am I getting old already, needing a rocking chair?* Almost thirty. That is not old. But the years were going by.

The first week of February little August gave his last tiny cry, his last troubled breath. There was a tiny casket in the house and the girls looked at it solemnly. Selma was glad for them not asking questions. They seemed to understand that the house was to be quiet, and only a couple of times did anyone have to tell them.

Ruth had told her girls little August was leaving them and they all cried for him, and Selma had told Christina and the two of them were crying, and when Julia and Anna came to Selma they told her about August so then Selma and all three of the girls were crying together.

Ruth could be up only long enough to listen to the pastor in the front room. For two days after the funeral the casket stayed on the porch while men took turns at the graveyard feeding a stinking fire of old lumber and rubber tires, thawing the frozen ground so the grave could be dug.

After that Otto had talked to Ruth long times in their bedroom, sometimes with the door closed, but often open. Selma could hear him murmuring to his wife and hear her hoarse voice with him. When he did talk to Selma it was always in the kitchen, always about what needed to be done, what needed to be bought, and he did not mention for a long time about her boys or what would happen if Ruth were gone.

Still, it was more talking than he had done in past years, and it was more as if Selma was part of the place. She understood this. And Julia, *Julia must see it,* she thought. The girl would stand silent in the kitchen, listening to her father explain things, listening to his questions. At other times when Otto was outside she would stand and look into Selma's face, silent still, just looking and looking, until Selma thought she herself should feel guilty about something.

In late February Mrs. Schloven was able to come again for a while, and for that time Selma did not feel right visiting with Otto. Mrs. Schloven said almost nothing to Selma for the four or five days, but later Ruth told Selma, "Mama says you are a good woman. But you should be firmer about the children." Ruth smiled at that. "Mama says that about everyone with their children." Ruth's words made Selma's life better.

The first week of March the pastor came to visit Ruth because she had not been able to get to church for a long time. After that visit the doctor came, and he told Otto, "She must get to the sanitarium as soon as you can go."

Otto was frantic. "I am a strong man," he said to Selma one night. "I am not saying that to boast. But I am healthy and I was trained well in many things and I am strong. Yet even that seems not enough to carry all these troubles. I cannot keep away illness and death from my family. And now she must travel but she cannot travel. How can I live with this?"

"I will have everything ready for you," Selma had told him. "Her clothes and toiletries, feather comforters, food, everything. The first warm day you must go."

"But even with that," he had worried aloud, "do I take the buggy or a sleigh? If it thaws quickly the cutter will pull too heavy and ride rough. If I take the buggy I could slide around in drifts or get stuck in mud. I can go from Edgeley by train up to Jamestown, but that takes money and somehow we would need to get from the train station out to the sanitarium. And if any of us go to the towns we will catch the flu that is taking so many."

Selma had not thought of the train. It always seemed such an extravagance that it should never be used. But now that he said it, she thought it was the answer and she told him so. She could see that with his mind the way it was, he could not decide for himself.

"And with the train you don't have to wait on the weather," she said. "There must be someone at the train station that can be hired to take you to the sanitarium."

But the flu. The war and the flu, and almost every family losing someone to one or the other. In church was the reading of the names of those lost, but those listening were fewer and fewer, staying away from each other because they feared they would be next.

With Ruth gone, Selma had felt guilty talking alone to Otto, and she waited until there were children in the room. At the same time she asked herself, *What am I feeling guilty for? We must run the household, we must do what is necessary for all his family. That takes talking.*

But at the same time she thought, *I am talking with him because I like talking with him, and God is watching like Julia.*

And Otto seemed to know, too, that something was changing between them. He missed Ruth terribly, and he talked about her with Selma more than he did about the farm and the house. But through that time he had not been silent as the first time Ruth had been gone. And gradually they came to talking almost every evening, most often in the kitchen while he ate and Selma finished cleaning up, but sometimes in the front room, she in the rocking chair, he sitting across the room on a straight chair, children with them.

More than once neighbors came. Selma would say, "Come in, come in," seat them in the front room, tell them she would get Mr. Wollerman for them, then go to her room, or pretend to be cleaning in the summer house. It looked too much like a family if she stayed. People would be gossiping, and what a terrible thing that would be for Ruth to hear.

More and more she had come to think of Julia and Anna as her own girls, just like Christina. They depended on her and there was now no one else to share time with them. It was not right, but she could not help it. If Ruth should live she would have to let go of them again, and that would be hard.

In June a boy on a lathered horse came from Edgeley with a telegram for Otto to come quickly to Jamestown. Otto was gone four days with no word. The haying had started, and Selma ran all day long, cooking for the hired man and the neighbors who came to help, getting food out to them in the fields, doing the milking and the barnyard chores, teaching the girls to weed the garden but keeping an eye on them, hooking the rope slings in the hay loads so the hired man could drive the team that pulled the loads up into the overhanging loft door.

"Where is Papa? When is Mama coming home?" Anna and Julia asked over and over.

Selma felt so bad for them. She had no answer, except, "They will be coming home soon," and even as she said it she felt guilty because she did not know what was happening, did not know if it was true.

On the fifth day they both did come home. Otto was pale, unshaven, his clothes the same as he had left in. He got the hired man to help him carry Ruth in a stretcher. They put her in her room again. Selma had the work of caring for her, listening to the coughing, the ragged breathing. Ruth was too weak to talk, and most of the time she did not know anyone was in the room.

"Mrs. Schloven will come to help again in a couple of days," Otto said.

And so in July the girls had seen another casket. This one they understood enough to be frightened. They clung first to Otto but he didn't seem to know them. Then they clung to Selma and she tried to say the right things but she didn't know what that would be, or how any words could possibly be right.

"Who will die next?" Julia had asked.

Selma could only answer, "We don't say those things."

A week Otto had worked almost day and night after that, until he was so drawn and exhausted he did not look like the same man. On a Saturday night he went alone to town and Selma heard him coming back Sunday morning early, clumsy in his walking, shouting at God.

She was afraid of him then, and she did not go downstairs. His noise woke the girls and they came to Selma's room frightened.

"Shhh," she said. "I think Papa is feeling bad because Mama is gone. We will leave him be."

"Mama should not die," Anna said. "I want her not dead."

"I know, I know," Selma comforted her. "Try not to think about it." The girls finished the night sleeping in Selma's bed, and she herself in her rocker, but not sleeping.

Otto had slept almost all that day. In the evening he asked for a bit of supper, and then went back to bed again. Selma did the milking and feeding without being told. After that, he seemed to become himself a little more each day, but never a happy man.

"Two deaths in the house in one year, a first son and a wife," he told Selma. "It is too much for any man."

But gradually again they had begun the conversations in the evening, and it had been in August, early in the harvest, that he told Selma to send for her boys.

She had been so happy to see them that she ignored the girls and Otto for days, instead trying to talk with the boys and cook their favorite things even while she was cooking ahead for when the harvest crew would come.

"I am so happy with my boys but I think I am being silly over them," she told Otto after a week of that. "And they do not think much of being with a woman all the time. They should go out and help with the field work."

"Yah, they can learn to pitch bundles," he replied. "They are big enough."

"But not at the machine, please," Selma had asked. She still was afraid of those slashing knives and that powerful, whining belt.

"No, just onto the wagons is good. Or they can shovel grain, or haul water for the engine. Everything helps."

But even this gets complicated, she thought now. The boys at first were afraid of Otto, and they learned from him quickly what he wanted done. After they had to start going to school they were not so afraid of him, and sometimes they were pulling tricks like they had done with Mutter. Once on a school day Otto had found them setting snares for rabbits along a windbreak a mile from home.

"That I cannot have," he told Selma. "They must stay in school and I am not one to let them get by with these things." Selma had scolded Rudy and Daniel and threatened them with a whipping, but she did not know if it would help.

She could hear the boys thumping on the floor now upstairs, so she put down the darning and went up there and told them again, "Get to bed now." She wanted to tuck them in as she did with the girls, but they were getting too old. Years of that she had missed, and now they did not want it.

They were good boys, but as Mutter said, they were boys. It would take some getting used to for all of them. She hoped the boys would come to think of Otto as a man to look up to, and she hoped he would be patient with them. It was strange for him, too.

It is strange for all of us, she thought again now. And if it went on a while more and Mutter must come, it would be strange even more. She had not dared talk to Otto about that.

And if it must end, then we must get used to that, too, she had told herself so often, but now, now with no one dying in the house and their lives still sad and so busy but at the same time nice the way it was, and she herself sitting here waiting for the company of a man who was good to visit with, she was afraid of that thought.

What I am thinking about Otto is wrong, she told herself, *and being in this house with him is wrong now, and God will punish me for this but I cannot think anymore of leaving. I want only to stay, for my children to have a home and some life for all of us and for me to be with Otto.*

She heard him come in, caught the familiar smells of sweat and the barn. While he washed his hands and face she set for him some cold ham, some cheese and dill pickles, white bread with butter, some bean soup she had kept warm.

He chuckled when he looked at the meal. "I remember this," he said. "The same meal as when the kitchen was full of pig guts last fall."

"Maybe I am reminding you it is soon time to butcher again," Selma replied.

She scrubbed the kettle and waited for him to finish eating. When she went to sit across the table from him she did not bring the lamp, so they were partly in the darkness.

"The children are asleep?" he asked.

"Yah, well maybe not the boys yet. I have told them twice. But they are quiet."

"I must come in tomorrow and see my girls for a while. I have been too much away from the house this week."

"Julia and Christina will be in school."

"Ach, I forget. In the morning I go out later then."

"The horses are working good for you today?"

"Yah, better every day. It takes a while for them to get in shape. Plowing is the hardest for them. When I own a tractor I think my horses will be wearing a big smile in plowing season."

He wiped his arm across his mustache. "Good supper," he said. "Best without the pig guts."

"A tractor would cost so much…" Selma said, and wondered why she said it.

"Yah, and a man must learn to fix them when they quit, and they are dangerous. But, for plowing they will replace the horses someday. So…"

Selma took a breath and interrupted him. "I must talk with you about something else," she said, and then quickly, "I think I must leave here."

He didn't answer, and she did not dare look at him, yet she thought she must look at him, and if he said leave she would do it, but it would be harder than anything in her life.

"Why would you...?" he said. He was looking in her eyes, looking as if he could not understand her saying such a thing.

Selma talked then all in a jumble, holding back nothing for the first time with him, for the first time since...she could not remember. "I am thinking it is not right to be in this house with you," she said. "Ruth is still here in my mind, and she was good to me, and you are her husband and I am not divorced. I am happy here with your girls, and this will be a good place for my boys and Christina, but we cannot live with you and I like this. It is not right. So I must leave, but...I do not want to leave. I do not want to leave you. Anna and Julia are like my children, too. But a man and woman not married cannot live like this in the same house, and married we cannot be and I am sorry to tell you I have even thought of that because it is not right..."

He interrupted her, saying, "Selma. Listen to me," but she kept on talking.

"So I must leave, and I have a little money saved, and if you would bring Mrs. Schloven here for a few days I will go to Edgeley and LaMoure and maybe Jamestown until I find a place for my children and me. Then if I could borrow a team and wagon, or I could pay you to move my things if you could wait until I am settled, but I do not want to leave...I do not want to leave, God forgive me."

"Selma, stop," he said, and this time she did. He reached across the table. "Give me your hand."

She was frightened by this. What could he mean? She told herself, *You are not fifteen years old, you have said everything, so now is the time to be the grown-up.*

But she gave him her hand. His was warm, strong, calloused, yet he held her hand lightly.

"I have not been in the fields until dark every day because I am so hurried with the plowing," he said.

"What are you saying?"

"I have been in the fields because I did not dare come in with you.

101

I…I must tell you I have given up on God long ago, but still I fear Him from my childhood, and I fear His punishment for what I have been thinking about you…and Ruth gone only a few months…and her children in the house. Every night when I come in I am hoping you will be upstairs in your room and we do not have to talk because that would be easier for me, and I have been afraid to tell you. So I am staying late in the fields because now…I am in my own house a coward. But please, Selma, do not leave…do not leave."

"But I cannot any longer be the hired girl here," she said. "Because of what I have told you. It would be hard to leave, but it is too hard to stay."

"Listen, Selma, listen. I am saying I have the same thoughts for you." His voice caught. "If you leave, it would be for me like the third death in this house this year."

"Otto, do not say such things to me if…"

"I say what I mean."

"It is wrong," she said.

"I know it is wrong, but we are here together, and we are not the ones that made it that way. I must have help and so must you. That is what started it, and now we are here. That much is not our fault. What we do with the feelings, that is on us, but even that we did not choose to begin. I have not forgotten Ruth. She is still…hurting inside me, especially when I look at the girls. I do not know if that will ever go away. I did not wish for her leaving, and I did not choose to begin thinking of you. But it has happened, and if God likes it or not I do not want you to leave."

"Since I was fifteen I am waiting…" Selma said.

"We must talk of the future, the future of Selma and Otto, not about leaving."

"Otto, please…"

"Be my wife, Selma. Be my wife."

"I am not divorced, and Ruth…"

"The one we can have fixed. The other…if God is what the preacher says, He will forgive. If he does not…I will not forgive Him."

"I am afraid to talk of God that way."

"Then talk of us. Stay with me."

"You cannot know how I have wished for that, even when…long before it was you."

"Then say yes. We are needing the same things as when you first came to work for me. You have no place to go and you need help with your family. I have no one and I need help with my family. That alone should be enough, but now I am telling you, there is more between us, and you are telling me the same."

"Yes."

"And we will make you my wife."

"Yes." She thought she would laugh and cry at the same time. "And no beatings," she heard herself say.

He laughed at that. "Only for someone who hurts you."

Still holding her hand, he stood and she followed, across the kitchen, across the front room into his bedroom, Ruth's bedroom, her mind a wild confusion of hope, shame, fear, happiness.

I left the dishes dirty and the lamp still burning, she thought. *Maybe God will look at that instead of at me.*

Chapter Five

The Reunion, 1982: Day Two

An argument had fired up, after the swimmers had come back and started listening to Grandma Wollerman again, but before the evening meal was started. The argument wandered around the house and yard, easy to hear but not easy to take hold of, like chasing a diving loon across a quiet lake.

It started when Julia, age 70, surprised everyone by muttering bitterly, "I've always said while my mother was dying in one room those two were in bed in the other room. I saw what was going on in that house."

It was not like Julia to be bitter or crude. She didn't say it where Grandma Wollerman could hear it, but Julia's sisters heard.

Granddaughters, grandsons, nieces and nephews heard about it, too, and mentioned it to their husbands and wives and significant others. In-laws mainly were a little nervous about stating an opinion, but as the afternoon wore on, even they forgot to keep their mouths shut. Julia's complaint took on several versions.

"Don't give me that 'victim' sob story," one of the middle-aged men said to his sister-in-law. He was dressed in blue jeans and a black Harley T-shirt, cowboy boots and bill cap, Navy anchor tattooed on his forearm, a beer in his hand as he straightened up out of the lawn chair. "That whining just ticks me off. Everybody's a victim except the white male, and he's always the exploiting chauvinist. Jeez, get a new line."

"Get a new line? How about you get a clue?" the sister-in-law snapped back. "Grandpa was older, this aggressive military type and Grandma five feet tall and maybe 110 pounds, with no place else to go. She had to be desperate. Look at it. She's stuck in his house. He exploited her. He seduced her. You could even say she was raped."

"Aw, that's just horse crap," the man with the beer said, and he stalked away shaking his head and muttering something about women's libbers.

A second husband, also perhaps less than perceptive, said, "It just goes to show you there was a lot more hanky-panky in the old days than they would let on. They just got all righteous when their own kids were starting to feel perky. And who knows? Maybe Granny was just a chippy."

"Now, that's really horse crap," his wife jumped in. "You just want to think that to justify all the running around you did in high school. They couldn't have been like you. The women didn't have birth control pills and the men knew it."

"And some people have a conscience," her niece added.

"A conscience?" the second husband replied. "It's like your aunt says. Dying in one room, screwing in the other. I don't see how a little youthful messing around is any worse than that."

"Is that what you told your own kids?"

"Well…"

The niece didn't let him answer that. "Not everything is as cheap as you make it," she said, and then she stalked away muttering about hoping somebody got what they deserved.

Two of Selma's granddaughters were almost shouting at each other before they finished their piece of the argument. "Julia's mom was dead for three months and she'd been dying for…a year or something. Sure, maybe they could have waited longer, but it wasn't like it was some casual thing, either."

"Oh, get real, sis. What's to say they waited even as long as she says.

Maybe Julia is right. But you just can't stand to think of Grandma as anything except this frumpy little old Bible-thumper."

"Well, call her a Bible-thumper if you want, but that's what she believes in, and she wouldn't have just thrown the Bible out the window just because the boss was horny. And she had had three kids in six years from her first husband, so it wasn't like she still thought it was something in the drinking water. Besides, look how many kids Grandma had all together. She must have got pregnant at the drop of a hat. So there's no way they were playing around before Ruth died. Anyway, Julia was…maybe six at the time? Seven? She sure as heck didn't know what was happening behind bedroom doors, so maybe she just has it wrong."

"She can't be too wrong. Katherine was born the next July."

"June, not July. But that still doesn't mean there was something…sordid…when Ruth was still alive."

"So why is Julia still bitter about it? She's not that kind of person about anything else."

"I don't know. Maybe she got it wrong. Maybe she looked at the dates, added two and two and got five, and never let go of it. These things happen. And they never would have sat down and talked about it. You know that. Or maybe she's still hung up on the fact that she's the only one not related."

"Not related by blood, but she's here, and she's part of the family. Mom says they were all sisters, that's what they always felt like."

"Yeah, but maybe there's more to Ruth than we know about and Julia isn't saying. Who knows? Nobody's ever heard anything about Julia's real dad."

"Right. So now you're accusing Ruth of hanky-panky but you're defending Grandma when she does the same thing. You can't have it both ways."

"I can think whatever I want. You're always telling me what I can or can't think. It's what you did to me when we were little and you've never quit. I'm just sick of it!"

"I never wanted to tell you what to think. You always asked, and I got sick of that. You couldn't make up your mind about…whether to

106

take a pee or not. You asked me everything. So I told you. And that makes me the bitch?"

"I didn't call you that!"

"But you wanted to! You just wouldn't let the word come out of your prissy little mouth!"

Finally one of the husbands said something right. "It's a family reunion, ladies. Keep it civil."

Not all the arguments came to anger and not all came to agreement, but as people got hungry they began to think of something besides Grandma's revelations. Later in the evening, when Grandma was talking again, some of the others built a little bonfire on the edge of the yard and sat there staring at it, beers in hand, tall trees at their backs, black mountains farther back, obscuring the lower part of the clear sky. There were three generations mixed together, the older two doing most of the talking.

The tattooed husband was among them, nursing another beer, not counting but he'd had enough to be pretty talkative. "I keep thinking about that farm life," he said. "Those old two-story houses were pretty much like what I grew up with. Hell, half of them are still there, the originals, just with a new kitchen added on and some wiring and vinyl siding.

"But the thing is, they were all about family. Yeah, in one farmhouse that might be all nicey-nicey, and the next it might be pretty rough. Anything could happen, but they had some ideal picture of family in their heads even when it wasn't going right, and I'm looking at Grandma, and her kids…" he looked around at those seated, "…some of you, and the next generations, and yeah, maybe some have messed around more than they should have, and there's been mistakes and divorces, but the fact is, there ain't a truly…bad person, somebody who doesn't give a damn about anything…there ain't one in the bunch."

"What about Boyd? Look what he did to Katherine."

"Yeah, but he ain't family. She had the bad luck to marry him. And she's still a saint after all that. And her kids are good people. So I'm sticking to my point. There ain't a bad one in the bunch."

"So what?" someone asked him.

"So I'm thinking that came from somewhere. Which had to be from Grandma, yeah, because she got stuck with the load, but Grandpa, he had to be…decent. Jeez, he already had one adopted kid before he met Grandma. Then he takes in Grandma's three, so there's five kids and only one of them his, before the two of them have their own family. That's a pretty noble thing to do. I think the deal is here we've all got this picture in our heads of these people from a half-dozen old photographs…nobody ever smiled, always in black and white, only thing they ever talked about is the weather, the crops, and the Bible. So we just can't picture them…you know, sweet-talking each other. Wanting to sleep together but knowing they had to wait, sometimes. Other times just giving in to the moment, to hell with the consequences, because…" he put his arm around his wife sitting there in the next chair, her face lit by the firelight, and gave her a long, long kiss, "…it was true love, baby. Just true love," he said.

Everyone laughed then, and a couple of them applauded. "Whooo," someone hooted. "Rudolph Valentino."

The tattooed husband raised his beer.

The wife said, "I wish I didn't have to wait for him to get through a six-pack to be like this," but she was hugging her husband and laughing with the rest of them.

Chapter Six

September 1923

Selma was transplanting some tulips for spring, and there were two neglected rosebushes by the porch. With some weeding and trimming and some manure, and maybe keeping them protected in winter, the roses might get going again. It was late to be planting flowers, but better than not planting them at all.

When they had moved from the Hubbard place the flowers had been Ruth's anyway, and Selma had just cared for them. The same on the Walters place, though there Ruth had died. Then the Thomest place, and now the Milton Dagel farm, but it looked like this would be a while, so Selma wanted some color around the place. And now, married four years, there was no longer any thought of things belonging to Ruth.

Selma was tired of moving, but each time was for better land, or lower rents, or better buildings. Plenty of places to rent, since the first homesteads were now forty or fifty years old, and with families changing, land bought and sold, some farms getting bigger while some went under, share-farming was good business, at least for the owners.

Otto was determined he would get ahead for his work, so he was always looking, looking. The Dagel place was south of LaMoure, 35 miles from the Retzlaff farm where Selma had grown up, where Mutter still lived with Henry and Emma and their babies.

"Ten years we can stay here, maybe more," Otto had said when he found the place for rent. "Dagel says he wants only a good job farming it. He wants the income without so much work, and it is not for sale. Maybe by then it will be, and we can buy it."

And the buildings are good, Selma thought as she loosened the soil around the rose bushes, digging wider and wider as she pulled up the endless roots of quack grass. Good barn, granaries, chicken shed, and the house is good, too. And big, and with eight children it must be big. But old, too, and maybe would be cold in winter.

A divorce had not been so hard. Something she had been afraid of for a long time, and when they went to the county it was just papers after all. Maybe different if Wilbur had still been around, but that he was not, and no one yet knew where he was. So, papers and witnesses, and that was that.

In April 1919 they had married, and in summer little Katherine had been born. By that time Ruth had been gone barely a year. They did not speak of her.

It had been a happy time, the best since Selma's childhood. Three babies and almost five years later it was still good, the unspoken thoughts of Ruth still with them, but Selma and Otto pleased with each other even with that.

"He does not like my big stomach," Selma had told Otto after they had visited the pastor in Edgeley about getting married.

"And I do not like his big stomach," Otto had replied. "Maybe he gets paid too much if he can get like that. Or sits too much in a chair looking down his nose at other people."

"That is why my stomach looks like this?" Selma had teased.

"No, I think your trouble is something with a man." He had laughed.

She had been with Otto that night in October when they came to understand that they must be together, and then no more for a while because Selma was so worried about it. But when her monthlies quit she knew it was too late to worry, so they had been together again in the winter, but always she had slept in her own room because of the children. Still, Julia had been watching, and still she had made Selma feel guilty.

Now eight children, so many that a day would easily go by and Selma did not know what three or four of them did all that time.

Rudy and Daniel were 15 and 13, both taller than Selma, lean strong boys old enough to be helping Otto all the time, and when they were not in school they did help, though it was not always good between them and him.

"I think they will never learn to work hard at what they are doing," Otto said more than once. "Everything I must tell them: 'speed up,' 'get back to work,' 'do that over,' 'that will never work that way.'"

The boys said little about it until Selma scolded them, and then they would argue, telling her, "He is not my father. What do I care? When I grow up I will get nothing from him after all."

"But you are my boys," Selma would answer. "And this is our life. And it is better than anything we had before I...before I married Mr. Wollerman. So you must do your part."

"What is my part with milking the cows?" they would ask. "I get no money for it."

"You drink the milk. You eat the butter. Now go do it before you make Otto angry again."

The boys had been in school enough to speak English between themselves, and they did it all the time, knowing Otto wanted them to speak German at home. It was one more way arguments would start.

"We will remember who we are and what we came from," Otto told them.

"This isn't Germany," Rudy would answer. "Americans speak English."

She did not like to see Otto angry at the boys, and she did not like to see the boys unhappy, but there was no more she could do about it. She thought that it was not easy for either of them. The boys have been without a real father too much and moved around too much. Otto has not become acquainted with them when they were babies, instead having them dropped into his lap half-grown.

But, a few more years and the boys would be on their own. That would make it easier for them and for Otto, too. And by that time little

Conrad and Fritz would be growing enough to be helping.

She had Fritz with her as she worked, just over a year old, still nursing, toddling around and falling down in the grass, wanting to eat dirt or worms or the shovel handle, so she had to watch him all the time. Conrad was easier already, running and talking good enough so the girls took care of him while they weeded the garden, picked the eggs, fed the chickens, churned the butter, washed the dishes. Both Christina and Julia were eleven, so they did much of the housework, and Anna was nine, so she was able to care for Katherine, who was four, and Conrad, almost three.

Six children she had had now. She remembered a photograph taken when Wilbur was still with her. She had been lean herself then, with a tiny waist even after three births, wearing a white blouse with big sleeves and tight wrists, a dark skirt with roses embroidered at the waist.

Even after I met Otto I could wear that, she thought. But not now. Thirty-four years old and six babies, and her thicker middle did not go away. But it was not so important now to have a fine figure and think of a man smiling at her as she smoothed her dress. Even the way she was, Otto smiled at her that way, and she was happy with that.

She finished with the flowers, scrubbed her hands in the kitchen, and took Fritz into her bedroom to nurse him. "You are soon done with this, little Fritzie," she told him as she rocked in her chair. "A few more weeks maybe, and then you will be mad. But you are getting too big for it."

And then what. Getting pregnant again? That seemed to be the way it was. As soon as she quit nursing, another one came along.

But she was lucky that way. Healthy. She could work the whole time she was pregnant, and the births were not so difficult. Then back to work, and so it went. Children were a blessing, and all were healthy.

Ten years they might be here, maybe more. What would it be then? She would be...forty-four. Rudy and Daniel would be grown men, Christina and Julia...what? Married by then? Selma would be a grandma?

It was hard to picture.

And Otto. Otto who was so strong, so sure he would be getting ahead all the time. He would be…fifty-one. Perhaps owning land by then, a tractor, an automobile for sure. That he would have soon, she knew.

And his children would go to school. "In every town is a *hauptschule*, high school, now," he had said just the day before. "There is no difficulty now to go to more schooling. They will all go, the girls, too. And there is talk of a bus to pick them up. Everything is easier, more modern. They must keep up with it."

Great plans Otto had. Always great plans. "I will not be a common laborer and my children will not," he said. "We will be landowners who do not ask others for work, people who do not take off their hat to the banker every year. The girls could be…teachers, or nurses. That would be something."

She shifted Fritz to the other breast, enjoying the nursing and the chance to sit down for a while. Some days the nursing was the only rest she had in daylight. But still she was hoping he would get full quickly so she could get started with baking bread. That was a constant task. Some days took two or even three loaves for so many people, and it was hard to keep fresh, so she had to bake at least once a week, sometimes twice. Soon Julia and Christina would be doing that, too, but still there was always the work, day and night if needed, even when the children learned it and took it over. And they must learn it because if they did not they would be helpless in the world.

When Fritz did finish nursing Selma went first to check on the beer she was brewing in the cellar. It was still raw and harsh to taste, but a few more days it would be ready. "What is life without beer?" Otto would smile. "A man might as well be a Frenchman or a Norwegian if he has no beer."

The Prohibition was on and Selma thought it was a good thing. It kept Otto from stopping at the saloon when he was traveling alone. But at home he still wanted some beer, and the batch working now was for a celebration. "New beer, bratwurst, and sauerkraut will we have to celebrate a new place," he had told her when he started the batch. "And the neighbors we will invite, so they can see this fine family."

Selma was hoping they could do that, if there would be time for it with the haying season. She had been to church, but only a couple of times and that was not enough to get acquainted. It had been enough to learn that this pastor was not looking down his nose at anyone. "Will your boys take confirmation?" he had asked.

"Yah, if they will attend," Selma had told him. He seemed like a person she could talk with. "I do not force them to it. They...lost their father when they were little, and they have had some troubles growing up. I will ask them and if they wish they will come. But in a few years the girls will come, I will see to that."

"I understand," the pastor had said. "I'll talk to your boys when the time is right, and then we'll just see, I guess. And your husband? He will attend?"

Selma had had to tell him the truth. "I do not think so," she said. "He is not happy with...the church, from his childhood in Germany. But he is a good man, a good father. Perhaps he will come when the Sunday School sings, but nothing more."

"Well, I will look forward to meeting him anyway," the pastor had said.

With Fritz banging two small kettles on the floor under her feet, Selma mixed and kneaded the bread dough, cut it into pieces for the pans, set it on the kitchen table to raise. The kitchen would be hot when she did the baking, but that could not be helped. The summer kitchen was not fixed up to use yet, though Otto insisted he would get it done when there were some rainy days.

Fritz started fussing, so Selma went to the stairs and called Anna. "Come change little Fritzie," she said. "I am baking."

A good place, this Dagel farm. Best of all was the soil, black and deep, as good as any Otto had ever farmed. "My father was always wanting this farmland, but he said the Norwegians had it all," Selma told Otto.

"Yah, they got some of it, but some of it was the first Germans. Your father was just too late, the same as me."

There was lots of wild hay to put up along the ravines and low spots. Cropland already planted, weeds not bad, a small field of alfalfa for

114

making the best hay for milk cows. Otto's plans for a dairy herd had not worked out on the farm at Edgeley, but maybe here. The creamery in LaMoure was taking in all the milk it could get.

A good place. Not so far from town. A pastor who did not look down his nose. A high school for the children. Ten years they might stay, maybe more. What would change in that time?

Perhaps the world would end by that time. In church was the pastor talking about the End Times, and Mutter was always one to talk of that, too.

Mutter would be with them, Selma was sure of that. She was almost no help to Henry and Emma now. Selma looked forward to that time. More work, caring for the older ones, but as long as Mutter could visit, as long as she could sing, she would be good company. It was Mutter's singing that Selma missed as much as anything.

And Otto in ten years?

He will be somebody, Selma thought. He was so sure of it, and he worked so hard for the family but always for himself, too.

Otto will be somebody, she thought again.

February 22, 1933

Selma tried to make the children keep their own outdoor clothes separate from that of the others, but that usually didn't work. So, each morning after she got the stove warming up and set out the makings of breakfast, she went to the unheated entryway and sorted overshoes, coats, scarves, and mittens into six piles.

It was quicker to get the children out the door if she had their things ready for them.

Finished with that she woke all of the children, sending Fritz, who was 10, and Conrad, who was 12, outside to help Otto with the chores.

Janey, Caroline, and John, aged 9, 8, and 6, got themselves ready for school, and Katherine, who was almost 14, got breakfast on the table. Some days Otto would come in and eat with them, other days he would come after they had started walking to school.

"Ten years this county has been talking about a school bus," Otto always complained. In bad weather he didn't eat until he had driven the children to school with team and bobsled. If the weather was not so bad and he had the time, he took them in the automobile. Most days, they walked.

Meanwhile Selma checked on Mutter, helping her on the chamber pot if she needed, getting her dressed if she was feeling weak, bringing her a morning coffee and a biscuit and then leaving her be if she was feeling good.

If the noise didn't awaken them, Elizabeth, who was 4, and Lorraine, aged 2, slept in until the rest had left the house. Once things quieted down, Selma would awaken and dress the two little ones, get them fed, then clean up the kitchen from breakfast.

"Mornings we live in a crazy house," she told Otto almost every day. *Too crazy*, she told herself. She barely knew the children sometimes, with babies coming all the time and sometimes so tired she didn't want to look at a child. Too crazy, and sometimes she knew there was too much shouting at them, too much hurrying, not enough laughing.

The older children were grown and gone, Rudy and Daniel working at other farms; Christina was gone, too, although it would not be long before she married George Holfer. Julia was away at Ellendale studying to be a teacher, and Otto was proud of her for it.

Anna he worried about. She had married Marvin Struther in a hurry, Otto so angry at them he had threatened Marvin with being arrested if they did not get to a preacher. Anna was only 18 now and already with a baby, but it was not that so much that bothered Selma. It was Marvin himself. He was not good to Anna, already leaving her alone while he went wherever he wanted, nasty talking to her, and him not always working at a job.

"I am sick about it some days," Selma told Otto. "It will be with her like it was with me and Wilbur Metwald."

"Yah, but I am so angry with her I cannot feel sorry," Otto had replied. "From now on we don't talk about it."

Long before daylight on this winter day, Otto told Selma, "I am going to bring some grain from the field bins. Some for feed, some to sell. First I go to town for a battery for the radio."

There is more he wants to say, Selma thought, so she didn't answer him.

"And I am checking for some tracks again," he added.

Anna was not the only child Otto was angry with. He thought Rudy or Daniel, or maybe both, had been taking grain from the field bins and selling it for their own money. Twice before he had seen tracks, and though he could not measure the bins exactly, he was sure some was missing.

"The boys are not thieves," Selma had told him when he was raging about it. "It must be someone else."

"Yah, could be, and I say nothing until I catch them," he would answer, "but I know they are getting money somewhere not from their work, and the tracks have been there."

"The wind has been quiet last night," Selma told him today.

"If there are tracks then…"

But it was another thing they did not speak much about. Too much worry, too much anger with it.

If only we had more money, she thought. Then losing some grain would not be so important. But money…what was that? Something they did not see very much. Cattle worth nothing, grain worth nothing. They had to sell grain to live, but the grain was so worthless it barely kept the farm from going under.

Selma often thought that they were back to what Mutter and Vater worried about. The bank, the bank.

And it was eating at Otto. He had always paid his bills, always been proud of people saying Otto Wollerman they trusted. Even with the bank, there had not been trouble borrowing, because the banker knew what was a good deal when it was sitting across the desk from him.

But dry years had come, and grasshoppers, and now the crops worth so little. If it did not change soon it would drive them out. Then what. They would have to quit farming and go to…

They knew nothing but farming. Otto could not live without land to farm, she often thought. He was too proud for anything else. It would make him a laborer, something his whole life he had worked not to be. And now he was 51, not an age to start over. And even if he could swallow his pride and work at something else, what would that be?

There was nothing else. The whole time on the radio the news was about the stock market and the low prices and people starving and no work anywhere, but the President always with "things will turn around soon."

At least on the farm they had food, even if sometimes they were wearing themselves out with digging the soil, planting, weeding, harvesting, preserving. Plenty of meat, too. Might as well eat the pigs and cattle. Selling them was for nothing.

Things will turn around soon.

Selma hoped that was right. Every day she was looking for something that said things were turning around. She did not want many more years like the last few, with Otto more and more worried, and sometimes now with drinking the bootleg liquor that made him wild.

More and more they lay in the bed at night without talking. More and more he did not turn to her and look in her eyes and touch her face and talk little foolish things, words that meant nothing yet meant everything.

Now it is back to back, worried both of us, she thought. But what could be said that would make it better? Nothing. So the silence between them.

At least the silence was not about Selma and Otto. It was about money, and children troubles, especially Anna because Otto thought so much of his daughters, and little things that children did every day, and maybe about Rudy and Daniel, too. But still not about Selma and Otto. That they had yet.

Good farmer, good to his wife, good to the children.

Some days he would put on a record of waltzing music and then no child was safe from him.

"Now we dance," he would shout, and pick up the nearest child and go dancing around the house. It was a wild game, because he would dance with one, then chase down another to dance with, all of them shrieking and giggling.

But now on the days he was drinking there was trouble, and everybody in the house stayed quiet, stayed away from him.

No beatings. He would never be that way. Just angry, and shouting sometimes, and scaring the little ones, and swearing and saying things that he did not mean. Then ashamed and better for a while. But then something would happen and he would be going after the liquor again.

With Lorraine and Elizabeth dressed and playing in the front room, the dishes done and the kitchen floor scrubbed, Selma sat down at the kitchen table for a little coffee. The wind was up again, she could see, and if there were any tracks in the snow they would soon be gone. She hoped this trouble was not what Otto thought it was.

Those boys, those boys, if only their life...

It was better with Conrad and Fritz, much better. They knew their father and he taught them as a father should. They were already working all the time they were not in school, and that was what Otto wanted, but he was not so hard with them either. In summer he let them go fishing, or play baseball in the barnyard sometimes, or swim in the river, or when the neighbor children came over they went up and down the windbreaks playing cowboys and Indians or catching mice in the rotting leaves.

This morning Selma could hear singing and knew Mutter would be having a good day, would maybe even come down and sit in the kitchen for a while.

Mutter was 80, very heavy, very slow, but cheerful yet. The most work she could do was peel potatoes or dry the dishes. She spent most days in her room holding her Bible, sometimes singing just as Selma had hoped she would, all the same hymns, and her voice strong and clear, not screeching and shaking as with some of the other old women in church who should quit with it.

Like a famous person on the radio, Selma thought. It is good to have that singing, good for the children to hear an old person still bring something good into their lives.

Almost ten years on this Dagel place, she thought, sipping the last of the coffee. Otto still had not built a dairy, and now...never, though he did not say it. For Selma, ten years of more babies...most days good, but work and worry never ending.

No dairy, and no owning land yet either.

And Otto had not become somebody yet. Not to his way of thinking.

119

Trusted by others, still putting up good crops and raising good horses, but time was getting away, getting away.

She herself was forty-four. Forty-four years and looking like a full sack of flour now, short and round and solid. Forty-four years, eleven live births, one miscarriage, thirteen children raised, or being raised, from twenty-four down to two years. No more looking in the mirror to smooth a new dress over a fine figure.

A new dress would be enough. The fine figure was gone forever, gone with her childhood, gone with so many other things childish to think about.

But eight children still at home, and a husband to care for, and her own mother, and a farm to worry about, and some things to get ready for the evening meal. No time to sit and daydream.

She hoped Otto was wrong about the missing grain, wrong about the boys. She did not want them to be like their own father, or like this Marvin Struther that Anna had married. She often wondered why there were men like that. Was it just from evil in the world like the Bible said? There seemed to be no end of them to marry girls that could not seem to stay away from them.

Liars and run-arounds and wife-beaters, so many of them, so many.

Yet there was Otto, not like them at all. And George Holfer…she did not know Christina's friend well, but he seemed to be a good man, kind to Christina and laughing with her.

What made the difference? Why would God let those evil men live? She did not know an answer. It was another thing she worried about, something she did not talk about with anyone, not even with Mutter.

Selma put her cup away and went to the smokehouse to get some sidepork. This and some fried potatoes, Otto would like that for supper.

She hoped the day might bring some better news from Anna, hoped Otto would not stay long in town.

At noon he did come in for a quick lunch.

"I see some tracks," he said. "I cannot tell coming from where. But some barley is gone I think, so I am to town going again to find out."

"Go ahead," Selma answered, thinking maybe now they would

know, but thinking, too, that maybe she did not want to know.

In the late afternoon she looked out and saw the children coming from school, Katherine walking ahead so she could pretend she was too old for the rest, Fritz and Conrad covered with snow from wrestling with each other, Janey and Carolina and John trudging along, tired from the walk. The days were starting to be a little longer, so there was still good sunlight for their walking. Snow like a wide river was flowing and flowing just above the drifts, across the fields, around the buildings, through the fences.

Otto had not yet returned from town.

Nice day, Selma thought, *but cold. And now time to get supper, and the boys must do chores instead of waiting for Otto, and the girls can get in some wood and then help me in the house.*

By the time Selma got the children to bed and went to her own bedroom, she knew Otto would be drinking somewhere. This was how it began...a quick trip to town, and then not coming home.

And the way it went was that she would not sleep until he was home, and if he was wild, she would get no sleep then, either.

She lay in the bed thinking about the same things she had in the daytime, the money and the children, the farm and Otto, good men and evil men and with men the liquor, and hoping some barley was not missing.

In church the pastor read from the Bible almost every Sunday, *"Do not associate with any so-called brother if he should be an immoral person, or covetous, or an idolator, or a reviler, or a drunkard, or a swindler—not even to eat with such a one."*

Sometimes she thought that pastor was looking only at her when he read it. "This is why prohibition is a good thing," he would say. "We should not be angry that the government has decreed it. Alcohol is an evil, and prohibition is merely carrying out the words of Scripture."

So it was that when Selma thought Otto might be drinking she left food on the table but she did not want to eat with him, even if he came home early, nor did she want to visit with him. If he was not disturbing the children she just avoided him.

All those other sins, those things were not Otto. *And he is not a drunkard*, she thought. *Not one who was drunk every day and worthless*. He worked as he had always worked; he thought as he had always thought.

Still, when he was drinking there was trouble. She could not pretend any different.

Alcohol was evil. Drunken men were evil. Otto…

No. He was not an evil man. Only he was a man who could not work hard enough to stop the years from going by, stop the long run of failing prices for the work he did, change the failure that was happening to them, but which he still never talked about, and which she certainly never said to him.

Still, good man or not, he was drinking, and drinking was evil.

The same thoughts went around and around in her head, and finally there in the blackness, she thought it must be nearly morning, she heard a motor, and she heard him come in.

His footsteps were hard, here and there, as if he was looking for something, stopping once at her door, but not coming in. *Maybe he will go out to the barn and not sleep at all,* she thought, *ashamed of himself, not wanting to show his face until he was sober.* Or maybe he would sleep in the front room. It had happened before, on the sofa or on the floor.

The steps came back and he came in, walking wildly about the room but saying nothing. He lit a lamp, then blew it out and left the room.

Selma re-lit the lamp and went to the kitchen. Otto was standing by the table and turned around when he saw the room lighting up. He was still in his cap, overcoat, and overshoes.

"What is the trouble?" Selma asked, though she thought she knew what it was.

"Nothing. Go to bed!" he shouted.

"You will wake the children with your shouting."

"Go to bed, woman," he said again, not so loud. "I must my family protect."

Selma realized the motor noise was still going.

"You have the car left running," she said.

"I am going to kill a man. It is nothing of your business," he told her, and he went out, a gun in his hand.

Selma went back to bed but she was fully awake, so frightened at his words that her skin was crawling. She lay for a while thinking he must have learned something about the grain and was going out to check, perhaps to catch someone. But still, she knew he had been drinking, too. A gun and the wild talk. She wanted to call someone for help, but who would that be?

A whole night almost without sleep she had, and there was nothing to do for it now. She got up again and dressed, stirred up the fires, started some water for coffee. The house was cold and she started shivering, but even when the stove warmed the shaking got worse. When the children came to eat they asked, "Where is Pa?"

"I think he had one of his bad nights," she told them. They knew better than to ask any more, and Selma was glad of that because she didn't know what to tell them, didn't know if she could even say words at all she was so terrified.

He came home again just as the children started walking to school. Katherine came in with him.

"I have asked Katherine to cook my breakfast," Otto said. He did not seem drunk, but something was wrong, that Selma could see. His face was white as with sickness, and when he sat at the table, his hands were shaking.

"I can cook it," Selma said. "She should be to school going."

"Katherine will do it," Otto said in return. "Please. I have something to tell you."

He jumped up from the table and went to the front room, his steps sounding hard as they had in the night. He was on the sofa for a while, then came back to the kitchen stamping the same, both hands waving at her.

"Come here, come here," he said, and turned back to the front room. "Something I must tell you."

She came and stood before him, but then he sat in the straight chair. "Sit on the sofa," he said, so she did.

He was not drunk now she could see, but he was wild still, and dirty, and smelling of alcohol. For a long time he did not talk, but sat looking first at Selma, then at the floor, then standing up, then sitting with elbows on knees, his face in his hands, twice groaning out loud.

"I must go to the sheriff," he said then.

"What has happened?"

"I am hungry and I want my breakfast. Then I will go to the sheriff to…to be arrested."

She saw now that his whole body was shivering, and when she saw it she felt herself so weak she thought she would pass out. She asked, "What have you done?"

"I don't know," he answered, standing again. "Something I think. I was home for the shotgun and I went back to town."

"I know you were here. We were talking then. Otto…tell me what has happened."

Again with his head in his hands. "I have shot a man," he said, almost whispering.

Selma thought she might faint. "You cannot…"

"A man who says what he said must pay for it. I held the shotgun. The window was broke and the curtain was moving. I do not know if I shot him. I must go to the sheriff."

He jumped up yet again.

"I will have my breakfast now. Then I go."

Katherine had set a plate and then left quickly for school. Otto began eating the eggs that she had fried, but he did not have to leave for town.

Instead, the sheriff and another man drove into the yard and took him away.

Selma could not move from standing in the kitchen. When little Elizabeth and Lorraine came downstairs, they took one look at her and began crying.

Only then did Selma herself begin moving, and that was to sit down on the floor and cry with the children. She did not know what else to do.

Chapter Seven

March 8, 1933
County of LaMoure
State of North Dakota vs. Otto Wollerman
In district court, third judicial district:

*Now comes A.G. Porter, state's attorney in and for the county of
LaMoure and State of North Dakota, and as informant here in open
court, in the name and by the authority of the state of North Dakota,
gives this court to understand and be informed:*

*That heretofore, to-with: on or about the 23rd of February, 1933, in
the city of LaMoure, the above named defendant did commit the crime
of murder in the first degree, committed in the manner following, to-
with:*

*That at said time and place the said Otto Wollerman did wilfully,
unlawfully, feloniously and deliberately, without authority of law and
with a premeditated design to effect the death of one Perry Hodgins
and with malice aforethought, make an assault upon the said Perry
Hodgins and did then and there shoot off and discharge at and upon the
said Perry Hodgins a certain single barrel twelve gage shotgun which
was then and there loaded with gun powder and leaden bullets and*

which said gun was by him, the said Otto Wollerman, had and held in his hands; and by shooting off and discharging the said gun aforesaid, so loaded with gun powder and leaden bullets and so held in the hands of him, the said Otto Wollerman did wilfully, unlawfully, feloniously, and deliberately, without authority of law, with a premeditated design to effect the death of said Perry Hodgins and with malice aforethought, strike the said Perry Hodgins upon the head and chest with said leaden bullets shot and discharged from the gun aforesaid, inflicting on and in the head and chest of the said Perry Hodgins diverse mortal wounds, of which mortal wounds caused as aforesaid by the defendant Otto Wollerman, the said Perry Hodgins died at the time and place aforesaid, to-with: at LaMoure, North Dakota, on the 23rd day of February, 1933, die.

And so the defendant Otto Wollerman did, in manner and form aforesaid, wilfully, unlawfully, feloniously, and deliberately, without authority of law, with premeditated design to effect the death of the said Perry Hodgins and with malice aforethought, at the time and place aforesaid, kill and murder him, the said Perry Hodgins; this contrary to the fore of the statute in such case made and provided and against the peace and dignity of the state of North Dakota.

Signed, A.G. Porter, state's attorney in and for LaMoure County, North Dakota
Witnesses: O.G., N.J.C., C.J.J., C.L., A.G., Selma Wollerman, A.N., F.D. L.L.

It is like banks and divorces, Selma thought. *Papers and papers, all in English with big words of things so confusing.*

When she heard them read she understood only the names and words such as "shotgun," "murder," "death," and a few more, and the sheriff said because of what Otto had said to her she should sign the paper, so she had done so.

Now she listened to the lawyers and the judge, and they were not much easier to understand than the papers, but what did it matter. There was Otto, shaved and his hair slicked down, wearing the old black suit

Selma had brought him in jail, but looking small and lost, his hands folded tightly in front of him when he stood.

She was feeling small and lost, too, terrified by what Otto had done, terrified at what would become of him and her and the family, terrified that people in town and all around the countryside knew what had happened and were speaking of it when they saw Selma come to town with a horse and sleigh, or in the car when Daniel or Rudy could come to drive her.

Terrified, but shamed, too, that their lives had come to this. Shooting a man, and making their lives so visible to everyone around them. She wanted to hide.

The courthouse was frightening by itself, a large, quiet brick building where people worked who could use papers to charge a man with a crime, throw him in prison, take away land and homes and children.

In the basement was the jail, cold but not freezing, light bulbs in the hallway but not in the cell. Otto had room only for a single bunk, a chair, and a pot. Selma had been to visit him only twice, and already she could see that being kept so close was crippling to him, a man who thought no matter what the weather, indoors was only for a meal and a quick sleep.

"The children are not sick?" he asked each time.

"No, just the sniffles for John and Katherine. The rest good."

"They are obeying you?"

"Yes."

"And the cattle?"

"We must talk of something more than the cattle," she told him.

"Yes."

"What is for money?"

"Only what you know in the desk, and what you might sell of grain."

"What is going to happen to us, Otto? We will starve without you, lose the place. I cannot keep eight children and all the farmwork. It was this way before I came to work for you, and I was younger then and not so many children. It is too much."

"Daniel and Rudy must come over to help you. And Conrad and

Fritz must take up the work. And Selma…you must be sure the boys do the feeding properly. We cannot have starving horses on the place. They would not be strong for spring work, and what would people think?"

What do people think of this family even with fat horses, Selma thought. *That the father has killed a man.*

"In the school the other children say things," she told him.

"Be sure they do the feeding," he would repeat, with his hands covering his face.

The courtroom was barren, with electric lights that glared from the ceiling, dark woodwork, pale green walls, hard pews across the back half, a set of twelve chairs and the judge's bench at the front. No one would come to such a place except from being forced. If it were not for the windows it would have been as frightening as the jail in the basement.

And as Selma sat at the back, she could see there were no others there just to watch. There was the judge, a man doing the writing, the two lawyers, a couple of deputies and witnesses, and pale, shrinking Otto.

When everyone was seated, the lawyer, Mr. Porter, spoke first, looking at the judge only. "If your honor please, in the matter of the state of North Dakota against Otto Wollerman who has been bound over from the county court of LaMoure county to the district for trial, and owing to the fact that our January term is still in session, I desire at this time to file a criminal information against this defendant, Otto Wollerman, and ask for arraignment."

The judge replied: "I presume, Mr. Court Reporter, that you will show that in the presence of the court is the defendant, Otto Wollerman, and his counsel, Mr. E.F. Coyne, and the court at this time orders the filing of this criminal information.

"At this time the defendant will be arraigned by the state's attorney reading the information to the defendant, and handing him a copy of the same. You may stand up, Mr. Wollerman."

The Mr. Porter then read from a paper aloud and gave one to Otto. It sounded the same as what Selma had signed.

The judge spoke again: "Let the record show that the defendant was arraigned by the state's attorney reading to him the information and handing to him a copy of the same. Mr. Wollerman, are you ready at this time to enter a plea as to this information."

Selma heard Otto reply, "I am not guilty." His voice was so weak it sounded like someone else, and she wondered how he could say 'not guilty' after what he had told her.

The judge: "You want to enter a plea of not guilty?"

"Yes, sir."

The judge again: "Very well, let the record show that the defendant at this time enters a plea of not guilty. The court is not ready at this time to set any date of trial but will determine that shortly. It may be that we will decide to call a jury and set the time for trial during this term. Is there anything further?"

The Mr. Porter answered: "Not in this matter, except I might say that I am about to request on behalf of the sheriff of this county to transfer this defendant from this jail to the jail at Valley City and I have the request for the transfer here."

The judge to Otto's lawyer: "Have you seen this application, Mr. Coyne?"

"No, I have not."

The judge again: "Is there any reason, Mr. Coyne, why Mr. Wollerman should not be transferred to the custody of the sheriff of Barnes County for a time pending trial?"

Mr. Coyne: "Perhaps no sufficient reason. I recognize the limitations of the jail here and I believe it is amply sufficient to keep this defendant in proper restraint."

What can this mean? Selma thought. *If they take him to Valley City I will never see him again.*

The judge again: "I feel that perhaps the facilities here really demand in this sort of case a guard here, and that is a rather expensive matter for the county to continue, and it is hardly right, perhaps, to leave a jail unguarded."

Mr. Coyne: "I will say in addition while we are speaking about the jail it isn't a proper place to keep anyone in restraint for any length of time without any exercise, it is not a humane thing to do regardless of the type of man kept there."

The judge: "We will sign the order then with the privilege of the return of the defendant in ample time for preparation for trial."

Otto was looking so helpless he was like one of the children. She wanted to scold him, take him home, comfort him with kind words, yet she was so angry with him. *What he has done to us, what he has done to himself,* she thought. *All with the liquor. Yet maybe it is God's punishment for what we have done together, Otto and Selma, when for a little while we thought only of each other and not of God's laws.*

When the deputy led him away, Otto looked back at Selma for a moment. She looked down at the floor, feeling so bad for him she wanted to break into crying, at the same time ashamed of him and ashamed of herself, too, that he might see in her eyes what she was thinking.

March 23, 1933

A few days after Selma had visited Otto in the Valley City jail, a letter came from him, the first one, something she had hoped for but feared, too, because no matter what it said there would be nothing easier, though she knew Otto thought he still was being helpful.

Getting to Valley City had not been easy. Rudy had driven the Model T, since Selma had not learned to drive it, but 60-some miles on rough roads was an all-day trip for a half-hour visit. Only twice did they make it, but Otto had told them of visits from others, too, friends who had not abandoned him. For days afterward Selma had been thinking about him sitting in the cell, bars holding him in, pretending to stand and talk like the old Otto Wollerman, but unable to stop himself from sitting down on the bunk and holding his head in his hands.

And that is what he did when she told him about Milton Dagel's visit.

Mr. Dagel had come as soon as Otto had been taken to Valley City. It was a visit Selma had known would come because the farm was in Mr. Dagel's hands.

"I am sorry things have gone the way they have with...with your husband," Mr. Dagel said. "And I am sorry that we have to talk about the farm. But that is the way it is."

Selma had set coffee and sugar cookies for him, and as they sat across the kitchen table from each other she thought, *This is my life, dealing with men who have more to do with my life than I do.*

"We cannot leave the place now," she told him. "We have no other arrangements, and we do not know what will become of Otto yet."

"I know, and I am not going to kick you off," Mr. Dagel answered. "There is a debt but spring is coming, and if the crops are good this year..."

"My older sons will help," Selma had told him. "And the younger boys must take over where they can. The hired man...if he will stay, or if we can get another one...so we can get the crops in without Otto." She was thinking of Vater when she added, "It has been done before."

"So we will wait and see?"

"The house is the most important," Selma told him then. "Eight children and my mother."

"The oldest is..."

"She will be fourteen."

"She can go to work then?"

"Yes, she will have to do that in the summer at least."

"So we will wait and see," Dagel had repeated. "I am only interested in getting the rents paid. About Mr. Wollerman..."

"There is nothing to say with him that makes a difference now," she had told him.

Before he left, he had said again, "I am sorry."

A good man, she thought of him, but he would not carry her troubles. They were too much for him even if they were his, and that they were not.

No, if anyone was to carry the troubles it was Selma Wollerman, that she knew. It seemed that God was only going to give her those distant few years of a good life. The rest was carrying of troubles.

For a minute or two she held the letter and stood looking out the kitchen window. It was like other spring days, plenty of sunshine, wind still cold but thawing, wide patches of mud showing, much of the snow gone but the biggest drifts still like strokes of white paint in rows across the land. *Everything is the same out there,* she thought, *as if nothing had happened, as if nothing in their lives made a difference. But in here, everything is different.* Otto was gone, and would not be coming back no matter what. The children were suffering for it in school, the farmwork would be suffering for it, the few friends they had were nervous now about talking to them because this thing, this evil thing was between them.

The first thing she noticed in the letter was that now with his troubles Otto was writing in English.

Affectionate Sweetheart Selma:

I am thinking right now about you and the children. God be with all of you wherever you go and protect all of you.

Now, darling, have you spoken with Keun about the money? What did he say? Keun and the witness will not come those days, they have no money for the gas and other hurdles are connected. He should come by him self. He said to me that the lawyer would do better if he would come by himself.

I do not know if he went today or not.

And I do not know either, Selma thought. Keun and another man had told Otto they would stand up for him at trial, and she knew the lawyer wanted their words. Otto had wanted Selma to pay their expenses but she had no money for that. She could not bring herself to tell him that.

Darling, I tell you one more time my best thanks for the hours, which you have given me. It is a sign of faith and love. God may keep you in the best health and give you peace.

And that is what I want, she thought. Peace. *But it will have to wait.*

Greet Mr. and Mrs. Torsen and I thank them for the visit. Greet Rebecca your daughter-in-law and the children. Tell them that I only did my duty. This man said many rough insults about you. If a strange person insults you, he insults me also. The children should not be mad at me, but should hold together. No matter whatever will come. They should join the church, it makes life easier.

Selma thought she had been telling him that for years. Now he was saying it. Why was that? Because he was feeling so guilty, or because he had fallen from his place of pride, what was it? Still, it did not matter what it was, because what he told her there took both father and mother to make happen. She would try, but it was one more thing to be alone with.

Darling, I dreamed last night about you, but it was not good. I tell you about this as soon as we come together.
Darling, I add another letter, put this letter in another envelope and send it to Miss Gaumer. I have to stop her mouth.

Missus Gaumer was a gossip, Selma knew, talking around the neighborhood and in church about what a horrible man Otto was, and how the family was no good and the children bad. Otto had heard it from more than one visit, but what good would a letter from him be? The woman would not change, and even if she did, there were others.

If it does not work out with the house, maybe you can the place from August Wusterbart use for rent and the boys have a lot of land around to rent.

Only a man would say that now, that all they had to do was up and move again for another place to rent. It was not that easy, not a plan for them, something probably they could not do at all, yet she could not tell him that. But that decision could be put off at least, as long as Mr. Dagel was saying he would wait and see.

Otherwise there is nothing news. Greet Paul Lenz. Now, darling, I beg God that he will you and the children bless with health, and give you a long life so we can see us all together. A new life would begin, so clean and clear as the sun is in the sky. Pray for me and let our Lord rule over us. Our Lord will protect and bless you in all your ways and give you peace. You have suffered enough, because of other people. Now, darling, I have to end this letter.

With affectionate greetings and kisses,
remains your loving man OTTO.

Maybe the lawyer Mr. Coyne had been telling Otto there was hope. Maybe that was why he thought they would all be together again. Or maybe it was that he must say that to keep himself from despair. But either way it did not help the family. Selma could see no hope for a new life of sunshine and peace.

Yet he was her husband, and a good man, and he knew that she had suffered. *And he loves me still,* she thought, and when they got away from thinking about the debts and the liquor and the silences that were between them, he sent affectionate greetings and kisses. She sat a long time looking out at the sunshine and the fields and the mud, holding the letter, crying a little, thinking how it was again that she was waiting, waiting, and again that she could not see what it was she waited for, except for Otto, and that was not possible.

You have suffered enough because of other people, he wrote.

And it was true. But his writing it did not make it go away, and if she felt sorry for herself that would not make it go away either.

She had to wait for whatever it was, and in the meantime she had to plan and she had to work. That much she knew.

April 6, 1933

A few more people this time in the courtroom. People to speak for Otto, or speak against him, and Selma knew she would be called up, too.

In the time in Valley City he had not changed for the worse. He still looked pale and small, not like a Prussian soldier, not like a man proud of his work. But at least now he was standing up straight and looking at the judge, not at the floor.

He is trying to look like something, Selma thought. *Pretending he has something left maybe. Telling himself he is a man.*

And she had been trying to pretend she was something, too, on the few times she had come to town, smiling at the store clerks no matter how hard it was, speaking to them as if nothing was wrong.

The children in school still had the worst time.

"My friends don't talk to me at all," Katherine said angrily some days. "I am so mad at Pa for what he has done. Why did he have to do this? Why won't they talk to me? It wasn't me that got drunk and shot a man. I'm not the one going on trial and being written about in the newspapers."

But other days Katherine was not angry, only hurt. She would come home and cry in her room, something Selma understood because she was doing the same, only not letting the children hear, she hoped. Late at night, not sleeping, staring into the darkness and worrying about everything, she could not help the tears.

It is weakness, she thought, *but I cannot stop it.*

The daytime was not as bad. Then she had work that kept her mind busy.

Mr. Porter spoke first when they were all seated. "If the court please, in the matter of the state of North Dakota against Otto Wollerman, the records show, I believe, that on the eighth day of March, 1933, the defendant was arraigned before your honor upon a criminal information, charging him with the crime of murder in the first degree, and at that time he entered his plea of not guilty to that information. I understand now that it is the purpose of this defendant appearing before your honor at this time to withdraw his plea and enter a plea of guilty to the crime of murder in the second degree and without stating reasons at this particular time for the state's agreeing to accept such a plea if that is the intention of the defendant."

Mr. Coyne replied for Otto: "On behalf of the defendant I wish to inform the court at this time he is financially unable to engage counsel. I have been acting for him as a member of the Bar to see that his rights are protected and have done that gratuitous, and I make that statement so that the court will take that into consideration. I might inform the court of his financial status."

The judge: "Are you satisfied, Mr. Porter, that the defendant is unable to employ counsel?"

Mr. Porter: "I imagine the probability that he is unable to employ counsel. However, I understand that Mrs. Wollerman is possessed of certain property, but as to its encumbrance, if any, I do not know. I presume its equity is small."

Selma felt her heart jump. Mutter's homestead quarter they meant. It was all to keep Mutter, its rents the only extra money. Now…now…did the lawyer mean to take it away?

Mr. Coyne: "I believe that Mrs. Wollerman has a quarter section of real estate, held in trust for certain purposes, the main reason being to support a mother. Otherwise, I think this defendant has no financial means with which to engage an attorney."

The judge: "The court will appoint Mr. Coyne for the purpose of this hearing."

Mr. Coyne: "At this time the defendant desires to withdraw the plea of not guilty heretofore entered, and desires to enter a plea of guilty to the crime of murder in the second degree."

The judge: "Mr. Wollerman, will you come forward please?"

Otto rose and stepped in front of the table he had been seated at. He stood with hands gripped behind him, looking first at the floor, then up at the judge.

The judge: "You are the defendant in this proceeding?"

"Yes, sir."

"Heretofore upon being arraigned in court you entered a plea of not guilty to the charge of murder in the first degree?"

"Yes, sir."

"Mr. Coyne is your counsel, and he now states that you wish to withdraw that plea of not guilty for the purpose of entering another plea. Is that true?"

"Yes, sir."

"Do you wish to withdraw your plea of not guilty?"

"Yes, sir."

"You understand, do you, Mr. Wollerman, that if you do withdraw that plea of not guilty and another plea is received that you will not have a jury trial, but will receive immediate sentence?"

"Yes, sir."

"You understand that?"

"Yes, sir."

"Is it your desire and wish to withdraw your plea of not guilty at this time?"

"Yes, sir."

"Very well, then," the judge said, looking at the man writing, "let the record show that the defendant's plea heretofore entered of not guilty be withdrawn. Now, Mr. Wollerman, that your plea has been withdrawn to the information, what will your plea be now?"

"What?" Otto's hands came unclasped and he shifted on his feet, turning once to look back at Mr. Coyne.

"What is your plea to the court now?"

"Not guilty," Otto said.

"That is the same plea as you had before. If you withdraw that plea, is that what you want to do?"

"Yes, sir."

"There is no need of withdrawing your plea if that is what you want to do. You better consult with your counsel."

On the wall the clock said ten minutes had gone by, but already Selma had lost track of what was happening. And Otto must be as confused as she was. He was whispering with his lawyer, first nodding, then shaking his head, then nodding.

This is what comes of him being so proud to speak only German, she thought. But she had more English than he did, and it was hard for her, too.

His lawyer spoke to the judge. "This defendant has great difficulty in understanding other than ordinary words. He is not able to grasp the meaning of the court for the moment."

Mr. Coyne looked back and forth between Otto and the judge. "Mr. Wollerman, you heard my statement to the court that you desired to withdraw your plea of not guilty to the crime of murder in the first degree and you desire to do that for the purpose of entering a plea of guilty to the crime of murder in the second degree. You said that?"

"Yes, sir."

The judge then: "Is it your desire at this time to enter a plea of guilty to murder in the second degree?"

"Yes, sir."

"You understand that, do you?"

"Yes, sir."

"Very well, let the record show that the defendant now enters a plea of guilty to murder in the second degree. Mr. Porter, how does the state feel about accepting that plea?"

"It is agreeable to the state to accept this defendant's plea of guilty to murder in the second degree. The state feels that in accepting this plea that justice will be served and that this defendant will be sufficiently punished. The state accepts this plea also for the reason of the age of the defendant, and the rules governing the service of this defendant in the penal institution, and that the state is protected sufficiently by the imposition of the sentence, which may be given by your honor."

The judge again: "I might state for the record that since I understood that this plea would be offered I have made some inquiry and I believe that the state is justified in accepting the plea, and therefore it will be the order of the court that the defendant be permitted to withdraw his plea of not guilty and enter a plea of guilty to murder in the second degree."

Mr. Coyne nodded and whispered to Otto. The judge began with questions.

"Mr. Wollerman, how old are you?"

"Fifty-one."

"Where were you born?"

"In Germany."

"How old when you came to this country?"

"Twenty-nine years old."

"You have heard from your family there lately?"

"No. I sent a letter and they never wrote me back."

"You are a married man?"

"Yes, sir."

"Have you been married more than once?"

"I was married twice."

"You have some family by your first wife?"

"Yes, sir."

"How many children did you have by your second wife?"

"Eight."

"This second wife is now, and was living with you at the time of the commission of this crime?"

"Yes, sir."

"Is your youngest child a boy?"

"He will be two next month."

"The two children by your former wife are how old?"

"Eighteen is the youngest one, the oldest one is twenty."

"Mr. Wollerman, you were brought up and educated in Germany, were you?"

"Yes, sir."

"What education did you receive in Germany?"

"Up to the eighth grade."

"And since coming to this country you have learned to read and write in this language?"

"I learned English to read."

"So that you could read a newspaper in English?"

"Yes, sir."

"What has been your occupation?"

"Farmer."

"What did you do in Germany before you came here?"

"I was on my father's place. I was farming there, too."

"Did you ever have any position with the government in Germany?"

"No."

"Were you ever in the army?"

"Yes, sir."

"How long were you in the army?"

"Three years."

"Were you ever arrested in Germany on any charge?"

"No."

"Were you ever arrested on any charge in this country before this one?"

"No. Never."

"Are you a citizen of this country?"

"Yes, sir."

"When did you take out your papers?"

"The first one in 1912, and the second out in 1918."

"Have you been voting since 1918?"

"Yes, sir."

"You came directly to LaMoure County when you came from Germany?"

"Except in 1912 I went back to Germany and stayed not quite three months and then came back to LaMoure County."

"You know if any members of your family ever have been arrested or in trouble?"

"No."

"Any of your children?"

"No."

"How did this happen. You can tell us in your own words."

Once Otto began speaking it was more words than Selma had ever heard him say. *Like a storm of words he has been holding in,* she thought, *and I have a storm of words, too, but I can never let it out.*

"The twenty-second of February I came to town and brought a battery in to Mr. Jorve and I wanted to see Dagel and I cannot find him and went home. In the afternoon I went to get some barley to put in, I wanted to get it home and put it in the bin and I saw some tracks, somebody been taking some out of the field, so I went home and tell the woman some is gone and I say I am going to town and she said go ahead, and I went to the elevator to find something out, if somebody sell some to the elevator.

"It was in the afternoon, five o'clock something like that before I left home, and I was stuck in the snow bank before I got to town and it was after five I start right to the west elevator, Andrews Elevator, and I walk in there and I see the manager from the elevator he was sitting at a chair and was awful drunk and was leaning in his desk and with a stranger man in a chair, and I couldn't do any business with him, and I see three half-pints of alcohol. I told the stranger man, I said, 'You must be a boot-legger,' and I told him to take that away somebody see that he will get in trouble.

"We brought the manager to the bed and I closed the doors to the elevator and the stranger man come after me and so I went to the next elevator, Mr. Larson, and I see him on the street and I ask him about that. He said, 'You can't do business with him,' and I come back to the car and the stranger man tell me, 'I like to sell out, I have some good horses and cattle and I like to sell out.'

"He claims there is not money in this place, so I tell him Mr. Dagel buying good horses, I drive with you I say, and we went up and Mr. Dagel in the bunk house and I tell him I brought a boot-legger, he like to sell out, what can you make with him a bargain, and so sat there a while and we was talk about the horses and he got two bottles of alcohol in his pocket, of course one was a little left.

"And afterward we went to Mr. Jorve and ask him about the battery, I like to listen to Amos and Andy and we start talking and the stranger man went to the door and said, 'Come on, Shorty,' and we went back to the elevator.

"We come to the elevator and he start to take a bottle out of his pocket and mix a drink of alcohol and water and sugar and I start to build a fire in the stove and then stop to drink there and he say, 'You must be the man with the two kids,' and I ask what two kids, and he said, 'Sure', and then he start to tell me that the kids was there last week and that is my step-sons, and they went to a party at his house.

"He said he wanted to sell his property and join Al Capone's gang he said, he start talking about the boys and girls. I said he should talk a different thing, and, 'You better hold your horses or I get mad.'

"He said. 'I like to work for you.' and I tell him I didn't want a boot-legger. He said I couldn't write and afterward he was through with that story he talk about girls and women the same way and we was drinking all the time and he want to fight once in a while.

"He started talk about the American Legion and Albert Winger raised up from the bed there and I told him, 'Shut up about the

American Legion.' He said Perry is his best friend and to come on give a drink and Perry give him a drink and I think that was the last.

"He talk pretty near a half hour before Winger found a dollar and Perry said he must get another drink and we went downtown and got some. I make the fire again and Perry starts talking I must be the bird with that two kids. He said, 'I get along with you.' I tell him I don't take a boot-legger. He said he wanted to sleep with that girl if he got a chance. He called me Kaiser and that didn't go with me.

"I said, 'You keep your horses,' and he pick that knife up. He say again what I do with the woman. I said, 'That is not your business.' He say, 'Kaiser, no get mad,' and he take the knife and he start to fight me and I push him back and then he say, 'I know where you live you better take me along or I will get after you'.

"He said he played cards with my woman, whist—my woman cannot play whist. 'Oh, hell,' he said, 'she play whist between her legs.' I said, 'You never mind my woman.' I said, 'You must be crazy,' and he said, 'I kill you just that quick with this knife.'

"I say, 'Man, you insult me because you call me Kaiser,' and he said, 'You go home and f--- the woman,' and I went wild and I went home and I never know how I get home. I take the gun and went back and want to protect myself and I went back and come over there and shot him. I don't know if I shot him. I don't know if I kill him. I shot—the curtain was flopping back and that is all I know. I went home, I don't know how I went home, and that is all."

From the time Otto finished telling the story until late in the afternoon, the questions went on and on. Selma was listening to them but she did not really hear them because all that time in her mind were pictures of drunken men pushing each other and talking foul, and Otto with the shotgun because another man had said those foul things about her, about Selma. She could not decide if what Otto had done, which was destroying the family's life, was a horrible thing, or if she should be proud of him for defending her.

But what good is honor if eight children are going to go hungry? she asked herself. And what good was this honor if all the other people knew nothing of it, knew only that a drunk had shot a drunk. And what good was this honor for the children to remember of their father, when the word itself they would not understand, but they would understand that he was in prison, and that other children and their mothers said things about him.

Selma was sick with the confusion of thoughts. She wanted to cry, to throw up, to throw things at Otto, to hide from everything, to go home and hold her babies, to tell the older ones life would go on, to tell them to shut up with the questions, to go to the front of the courtroom and hold in her arms a broken Prussian farmer, and maybe to shake him until his teeth rattled and shout at him, "Look what you have done!" and maybe to shout at everyone else, "Stop with the questions! Stop looking at us!"

The judge asked Otto: "You are quite a hand to drink, aren't you, Mr. Wollerman?"

"Yes, when I come to town and I get a chance I take a drink."

"When you get under the influence or when you get to drinking alcohol how does it affect you?"

"I drink too much I get wild."

"You get wild?"

"Yes, sir."

"Do you know what time in the night you went back to your farm to get a gun?"

"No, the whole night look to me like a few hours."

"Was it morning?"

"I don't know. It was dark."

"Did any of your family see you when you came home?"

"I don't know."

"Anything said to the family?"

"I don't know if I did or not, I got it in my mind I protect my family."

"Were you lying down in the house when you was arrested?"

"I wanted to come myself up. I don't know if I kill him, I thought I should go myself up."

"You knew that you had done something?"

"Yes, sir."

"You thought you should go and see the officers about it?"

"Yes, sir."

"Mr. Wollerman, did you ever threaten to shoot people before?"

"No. Never in my life."

"You used to treat your family pretty rough at times? When you was drunk you would treat them rough?"

"When I come home everything gets on my mind and I get in an argument with the woman, that was all I guess."

"And when you get that going you have no control of yourself?"

"I lose absolute control of myself."

"I guess that's all for now, Mr. Wollerman. You may be seated for a while."

After that there were questions for Albert Winger, the elevator man, mostly about the drinking and the arguing, about Perry Hodgins' nasty talking. Selma could not understand why it was being asked, because Otto had told it all. Otto's lawyer asked questions, too, from this Albert Winger, and some of that made the man a liar, a man who had been drinking and falling asleep when he was supposed to be working. What Selma could remember from it all was a picture in her mind—glass breaking, a gun barrel through the window, a curtain flopping back, and Albert Winger saying he saw Otto with the gun.

Then it was the doctor who had examined the body of Perry Hodgins, and after that a woman who lived next to the elevator, a Mrs. Hurley, who insisted she had seen Otto get out of the car on the passenger side, which confused everything even more.

"Which side did the person get out of?" Mr. Porter asked her a second time.

"The right side of the car."

"What did you observe after you saw the car?"

"I saw a man go to the window and break that and the shade was torn and from the light in the office I could see the barrel of a gun."

"Did you hear the gun discharged?"

"Yes, sir."

"What followed that?"

"Then the man ran back to the car after the shot."

"Do you think there was more than one person there?"

"I did, but I am not sure."

"What side of the car did you think you saw that person in the car?"

"The right side."

Nothing came of that except to make Selma wonder if Otto had help and was lying about it, or if he did not remember. Next was the sheriff, who had another strange thing to tell.

"What did you find concerning the telephone?" Mr. Porter asked him.

"The man that was working there told me he had cut the ground rod on the telephone."

"Mr. Wollerman had?"

"Yes, sir."

Again, nothing came of it with the lawyers, but Selma could not think why Otto would do that, even in the wildness of his drinking.

She did not have time to figure it out, because she was next. She walked to the front, her own steps sounding loud in the hollowness of the room, her heart sounding the same in her ears. She was afraid of the questions, afraid of the judge. *Forty-four years old and come to this,* she thought.

Otto's lawyer questioned her first about her name, her marriages, her children, and the place the family was living. Then "Who is doing the work for you on the farm at the present time?"

Of course she had to answer, "The two oldest boys," but it was embarassing to tell that boys 12 and 13 must do all the work.

When he came to asking about Otto's wildness she was embarassed then, too.

"Where did you see him?"

"He came in the bedroom."

"Did he say anything to you at that time?"

"He didn't say much. He was nearly wild. He walked back and forth and blew out the lamp and lit it again and picked up his guns and said he was going and kept on like that."

"Do you remember of his saying anything to you at all?"

"He said he was going back and kill this man and he was doing this on account of his wife and family. He would protect his wife and family."

"Did you know Perry Hodgins yourself?"

"No, sir, I never saw him."

"Had you heard of him before?"

"I did, I couldn't think of the name on account of the children and I told them when they got up and my oldest daughter said don't you know we had a party there. That is all I know the name."

"When your daughter said she had been there who was she with?"

"With her brother."

"When did you next see Mr. Wollerman that morning?"

"It was maybe six-thirty, like that."

"Will you describe his actions and what he said?"

"He didn't say much but he was wild and he asked for coffee and a little breakfast and the fourteen-year-old girl fried a couple of eggs and he didn't sit down and was just walking."

"Did your husband appear to be under the influence of liquor when he came to the house the first time?"

"I think he had plenty."

"How did he appear the second time?"

"He was wild that is all I can say."

"You said he had some breakfast there, did he say anything about going to town?"

"Yes, he said he was going back and see for himself. He had done something he had to come back."

"Had your husband been drinking very much during the past year?"

"The last eight years he did quite a little."

After that it was Mr. Porter with the questions to Selma.

"Mrs. Wollerman, what have been the relations out there so far as your husband and you are concerned, quarrelsome or not?"

"With the family?"

"Yes?"

"We had some arguments when he was drunk and he was a nice father except when he drinks."

"Did you see him take a gun?"

"Yes, sir."

146

"Do you know where he got the shell?"

"He usually had them in the desk and sometimes he had them in different places so the children would not get them."

The little bit of time with the questions left Selma exhausted and shaking. She went back to her seat feeling more and more lost. None of the questions to her or anyone else seemed to make any sense. Otto had killed a man. He told them that. What else could they say? Then they were going to call Mr. Jorve, the implement dealer, which was going to be worse because the bill was not finished there. *Otto is going to prison for murder,* she thought. *Why must he be punished even more about his bills?*

Mr. Coyne did the questioning on this man. "How long have you known Mr. Wollerman?"

"Since he moved here. I don't know."

"That is about 11 years?"

"Yes, sir. About that."

"Have you had any dealings with him during the last eleven years, business dealings?"

"Yes, sir."

"Have those business dealings extended for the full period of eleven years?"

"Yes, sir."

"From your acquaintance with him, Mr. Jorve, what would you say in regard to his character so far as his truth, honesty, and integrity is concerned?"

"I think it is all right, he done everything he agreed to always."

"Has he been prompt in meeting his obligations to you?"

"Yes, sir."

"Have you ever found him to be quarrelsome?"

"No, sir."

"So far as you know, what is his reputation as a law-abiding citizen?"

"Good."

"Have you observed the manner in which he conducted his farming operations?"

"Yes, sir."

"What would you say as to the manner in which he conducted such operations, as to his industry?"

"Very good."

"And what would you say as to his reputation as a farmer in this community?"

"Good."

"That is all."

Immediately then came Mr. Dagel, the landowner. By that time Selma was almost allowing herself some hope. She could see what Mr. Coyne was doing now, having people tell what Otto was when he was not drinking.

Maybe now they will see, she thought. *He is not a drunk, not a murdering man .*

"How long have you known Mr. Wollerman?" Mr. Coyne began.

"He has been on my farm since the fall of 1923."

"Where is that farm?"

"Five miles west and one mile south. He has been farming the three quarters of mine and he has been farming the whole section."

"What would you say as to his industry as a farmer?"

"Very good."

"What would you say as to his character for truth, honesty, and integrity?"

"Very good."

"Have you had a chance to observe the manner in which he provided for his family?"

"I have had several meals there and they are good."

"Have you noticed anything a little different or out of the ordinary about Mr. Wollerman in his business dealings during the past year?"

"Yes, sir."

"Will you state what that was that you noticed?"

"He seemed to be very nervous and worried about his debts."

"Do you know what his reactions were to securing a statement of account from a creditor?"

"It made him awfully excited."

"Do you know what his reputation has been in regard to paying his obligations prior to the last year?"

"Very good."

"Do you know whether he has been in debt to any extent up to the past two years?"

"Not until two years ago, maybe it was last year."

"What would you say as to his character and reputation as a farmer in this community?"

"He was a good farmer."

When the other lawyer asked questions of Mr. Dagel, Selma wondered if it was to turn around the picture, but it was not, and that left her wondering some more.

"Mr. Wollerman was a man who worried a great deal when he could not pay his obligations?" Mr. Porter asked.

"Yes, sir."

"When he promised some debt that he wanted to pay that would cause him to worry?"

"Yes, sir."

The judge told them they would rest for ten minutes. During that time Selma stayed in the women's room. She did not want the men walking past her seat in the courtroom and looking down at her. She did not want to go back in and waited until she was sure it was ready to begin. *Now it comes*, she thought. No more questions, only the answer from the judge.

Mr. Porter was given first chance to speak. "I have been personally acquainted with this defendant since he came to LaMoure County," he said. "I can readily agree with the persons who have taken the stand and testified as to the honesty and integrity and his ability as a farmer and his general reputation in the community. It is because of these things it is difficult to think or realize that this defendant is charged with this serious crime.

"One cannot, however, in the performance of his duty let his personal matters interfere with what he may believe. The state is justified in asking the court in imposing sentence upon this defendant that the extreme penalty be imposed…but it is not necessary that ten, or twenty, or thirty years should be meted out for the crime which he has committed, because I am satisfied that a short or long sentence would be more than punishment for this crime.

"The facts as found out by the state prompts me in saying that the state feels that in this case the court should impose the extreme penalty."

He is lost, Selma thought. *Mr. Porter is saying Otto is a good man but the extreme penalty anyway.* It would be more than prison…the death penalty. The room began moving around her and the voices became small and distant.

And he said more. "I realize the matter of the sentence that will be imposed and is as it should be entirely in the discretion of the court, but I urge the court the same as I would in this matter if there was a jury in which I would ask for the state the extreme penalty of the law."

If Mr. Coyne could not soften the judge's heart, Selma knew, Otto would die, and she herself could not live with the shame that would stain the family.

"May it please the court," Mr. Coyne said. "I desire to make certain other disclosures, which would have been made by witnesses had they been present here in the courtroom.

"The defendant had in his employ a young man by the name of Leo Glasser. He would testify that this man was a very good father, and that he took good care of his children, provided for them well and was kind to them. He would also testify that he did have some disputes and arguments with Mrs. Wollerman, mostly because of the two older boys, step-children, that didn't agree how, or in the way in which the work should be done.

"Another witness would testify to the past career of the decedent, Perry Hodgins. It appears that a few years ago he forced a young man to get in a car with him and he had a gun and forced this young man to drive him some distance for purchasing some liquor, and later this man Hodgins made threatening advances and the father of the boy took the gun and still has that gun in his possession.

"In addition it appears that Perry Hodgins was addicted to the use of intoxicants, and while under the influence was very quarrelsome and abusive and in company with other men he became very rough in his language and did things to rouse the anger of the other men.

"You have heard the story that Mr. Wollerman tells about the talk he and Perry Hodgins had. It is a most sordid kind of talk. It is the sort of talk that would inflame anger and passion in any man. There was no justification for it. It was a vile slander and Mr. Wollerman resented and said he was insulted by the words and the manner in which they were said.

"Your Honor will recognize that this defendant was born over in West Prussia, in Germany. Not only that his record was a good one while in the army but over there those men had a certain code of honor, and they resent any reflections on the family and most especially on the woman members, and when Perry Hodgins made the remarks that he did he was saying it to a man that would be very easily influenced even had he not been under the influence of liquor.

"Mr. Wollerman went completely out of control. He left the elevator with his temper aroused. I do not think that he is trying to hide a thing. He doesn't recall some of it. Something had sprung his mentality beyond control by the passion and anger and no doubt the liquor that he had drank that that reason had flown entirely away from him."

"I think that Your Honor can safely feel assured that this defendant is telling to the best of his ability everything that took place. In fact it is a tragedy and it is costing him dear. It is unnecessary for me to point out the position of his family and what they face under these times and conditions by having their father placed under restraint by the state.

"His wife suffers the loss of a husband. She needs his services at the present time and the home-life has been taken, and all I can say in conclusion to Your Honor is that it is just another mark, and a mighty black mark at that, written by alcohol."

And finally it came back to the judge.

"Mr. Wollerman, will you come forward?"

Otto stood and approached the bench. *Still trying to save something,* Selma thought. He was standing straight up and looking ahead, hands at his sides like a soldier, but even from the back of the room Selma could see that he was shaking.

"Have you anything to offer, anything further to say before judgment is pronounced against you?"

"No."

"It is not a pleasant duty that I must perform in pronouncing judgment and sentence, yet it is a duty I must obey.

"In pronouncing sentence I am taking into consideration your past character. I do not think there is any doubt but that your business career in the community has always been honorable. The reason for your downfall has been, probably, two-fold. In the first place you probably possess a temper, and when that temper got the better of you for that time, reason and judgment fled, and you were filled with passion. I presume in that state of mind you did do things, which now you cannot recall.

"The other reason is no doubt as it was pointed out by counsel for the state and your own attorney for the record, alcohol. Men say that more crimes have been placed either directly or indirectly to alcohol than any other place.

"The Court realizes that perhaps there is no doubt that this crime would not have taken place had it not been for the combined forces of these two things, and yet of course, that does not excuse the crime. A life has been taken, and that is the most serious offense against society.

"It will be the judgment and sentence of the court that you, Otto Wollerman, be confined in the state penitentiary at Bismarck, North Dakota, at hard labor, for an indeterminate period of 15 to 25 years."

The bang of the gavel was to Selma as final and deadly as a shotgun blast.

Otto was led away. He looked back at Selma once. This time she was looking at him, too, her eyes blurred with tears, one hand holding onto the next pew, her mind saying *No, no, please*, but her voice saying nothing. She did not know how much time passed. She was alone in the courtroom for some of it, and then a deputy came in and said, "Mrs. Wollerman, you must leave now. We are closing the building."

She walked slowly to the car. Rudy was there waiting in the fading daylight. "I didn't want to bother you," he said.

"15 to 25 years," Selma said.

"Yeah."

Rudy went out front and cranked the Model-T. It sputtered into life and they chugged along down the street, Selma thinking everyone there must be staring at her.

"15 to 25 years," she said again, and after a while, "So, we wait."

But this waiting would be different than any other she had done, she knew, because even if it came to an end in 15 years, Otto would not begin again.

Whatever is left from now on is up to me, she thought. *I will wait for Otto, but that does not mean I am waiting for him to make us a life. That is for me.*

Chapter Eight

Reunion: 1982

Something odd was happening.

Instead of arguments, now there were theories proposed and bits of evidence dragged up from individuals' lives, re-examined in the light of new information from others' lives, and set into place where they made a clearer picture. It wasn't that Grandma Wollerman was telling it all. Now they were all telling, though some still reluctantly.

In fact, Selma was spending more time answering questions than story-telling.

"Now I know why Lawrence Jarvis kept coming over to play cards after Pa went to prison," John said. "It was his way of standing up for Pa."

There were still two camps, two sides with potential for argument. One side wanted all the details, the whole long story, while the other side still said it was best left in the past. But they stayed relatively civil because that second side could see they were not going to win.

Those who wanted to hear it all tended to be younger or further removed in distance. "My God," a grandniece from Portland said. "This is fascinating. Why hasn't anyone talked about this before?" This was the side, of course, that asked so many questions that the other side

154

was dragged along. And, truth be told, the reluctant side wasn't exactly slamming the doors.

So while the arguments died down, a generation gap stayed alive. If Selma was the first generation and her children the second, then the gap was between the second and the third.

The fourth really didn't care. They were too young to pay attention to what was going on, though they listened to bits and pieces, reluctantly, when they were called to a meal. The fifth didn't care, either. He was the only one of that category anyway, and all he wanted out of it was to keep finding adults that could be trained to pick up the pacifier he was flinging across the room.

The third-generation sisters who had been at each other's throats over Grandma Wollerman's first bedding with Otto were chattering steadily now as only two women can do, both speaking at once, each on a different topic, yet each understanding the other.

"I'd always just heard that two husbands left her..." one was saying.

"That trial wasn't really a trial, you know..." the other began.

"...but this wasn't abandonment, this was something a whole lot deeper..."

"...and if he'd had a good lawyer, like nowadays, and a jury..."

"...drunk or not he was like John Wayne or somebody. This is that..."

"...and what about another man in the car, what was that?"

"...man's gotta do what a man's gotta do stuff..."

"...and cutting the phone line? Is this for real?"

"...which I've always said is a crock, but now I don't know..."

They were driving their husbands crazy.

Daniel, the oldest still living of Selma's children, got to be the center of attraction for a while. "I was working away from home," he protested. "I didn't know what all was happening over there at that place."

But he was still peppered with questions as long as he didn't clam up. "Yeah, I didn't get along with Wollerman," he said more than once. "He had all these big theories about farming, but he didn't want to cut me and Rudy in on the profits, so we tangled. And we were young

155

bucks, you got to remember. And he wasn't our dad. What do you expect? This stuff should be left alone. It was a long time ago."

One of the younger men was packing his car, getting ready to leave, and he made the mistake of saying something about jailhouse conversions and post-mortem idealizing. Word got around of that, and word got back to him before he could escape.

"There's a transcript of the trial," he was told. "In the courthouse at LaMoure. One of the nephews...he knows the thing almost by heart because he used it for a term paper in high school. You can't argue with a trial transcript."

"Come look at these letters," someone else told him. "They're downright touching. Hard-nosed drunks don't write this stuff."

And that subject of Otto was where the whole thing got as close to argument as it would get.

"I still say he doesn't have enough redeeming qualities to even come close to covering what he did," one sister-in-law said, and a few others agreed with her. "I mean, he spent all day drinking. He could have left at any time. He's in this filthy room with a couple of other drunks, and they're talking that...you know, locker-room stuff, and fighting with each other and just falling down drunk, and it isn't like finally Otto called him out in the street for a fair shoot-out. Jeez, sneaks up and shoots him through the window. Where's the heroics in that?"

But the tattooed husband once again said things nobody disagreed with, this time without the aid of a six-pack.

"You can't get bogged down in the details of his tactics," he said. "Look at the bigger picture. Here's this stand-up guy that knows he isn't making it...financially. Hell, in 1933 people were committing suicide all over the country for the same problems he was having. So he knows that, plus he's drinking, and it's hard to say which is cause and which is effect there. But you've got to consider the stuff they were drinking, too. I mean, that was rotgut. That stuff would make anybody crazy. And not to cut him any slack, it's plain he'd been at that stuff too much, and he was probably having blackouts with it.

"Then you throw in the insults to Grandma, and like the lawyer said, this is a Prussian soldier, too. Code of honor, if anybody even knows what that is anymore. So there's enough all together that he just cracked. After that the methods don't count for much."

"We've got to have more of these reunions," his wife said. "Last night he's a romantic, today he's a psychologist."

"How to get in touch with your inner self," he told her. "Step one, go to a family reunion."

"The thing that will surprise you if you ever read that transcript," the nephew told them, "is that even the judge and the prosecutor didn't want to convict him. They both hemmed and hawed about it. That tells you more than anything what kind of man he was."

"I've got to get a copy of that," about ten people said at once.

But once more the tattooed husband had them all nodding. "Before you go getting all excited about resurrecting Otto, you better remember Grandma," he said. "She's the one that's here. Let's don't go galloping off into the sunset with this…Prussian hero and forget what he left behind."

Chapter Nine

September 1935

It was a Saturday morning. Elizabeth was back in just a few minutes, crying her eyes out. "Gladys' mom won't let me play," she sobbed. "She said go home, your father is a jailbird, and Gladys can't come over, and I'm not spose to talk to Gladys in school anymore."

It wasn't the first time Selma had heard a thing like this. And wouldn't be the last, probably. Time might fix it up, but how much time? Too much for these children. They were hurt by it and they would be grown up long before people forget. Or forgave. And the same people sat in church and heard the word "forgiveness," but they didn't think what it meant.

"You will find another friend," she told Elizabeth. "You don't need to cry about these things. Somebody else will be your friend."

"What's a jailbird, Ma?" Elizabeth sniffled. She was six years old, knowing things about her father, but forgetting them, too, in two years going by.

"We don't say that word. That woman does not know what she is saying. Maybe we should..." She took Elizabeth by the hand. "Maybe we should wash out that woman's mouth with soap, what you think of that?"

Elizabeth giggled. "For a naughty word," she said.

"Yes. Then she would stop that," Selma told her.

"But I want Gladys for a friend," Elizabeth said again. "She showed me her dolls."

"How many girls in your room in school?"

Elizabeth counted on her fingers, missing one, starting over twice, coming up with nine.

"See," Selma said. "Lots of girls. Somebody will be a friend."

She hoped it was true. She hoped it was true for all the children. New school, new town, she hoped maybe people would not think about Otto's troubles.

But she knew better, too. Grand Rapids was only seven miles from LaMoure. Same newspaper, same county seat.

It had been worse for Katherine, now 16, old enough to…old enough to be thinking about a boy, old enough to be hurt in ways she would not grow out of.

At 16 I was looking at Wilbur Metwald, Selma thought. *See what that did.*

With Katherine it had been a boy at LaMoure, two years older, nice boy from a big farm. John Stennes, friends with Katherine since walking to grade school.

"I think we will be married," Katherine had said this past spring. "We have talked about it."

It had taken Selma by surprise, but she should have known. Katherine was unhappy at home, that was plain. She was old enough to be thinking of a life for herself, and there was too much work taking care of the little ones, too much hearing "there is no money for that." And she was growing into a woman, short like Selma, fine bones, dark eyes, small waist, strong, and liking to laugh. Men would like her.

"You must listen to me about that," Selma had told her. "Men are men. John seems like a good man…boy. But do not give yourself to him. Your father has given us more shame than we can live with. If you…"

Katherine had replied, "I know what you are talking about. You do not have to tell me anything."

So independent then, Selma thought. *But a few days later, crying and crying, refusing to go to school, refusing to talk, to eat.*

Finally Selma had had enough. "Tell me what it is," she had said. "We cannot have this foolishness you are doing."

And so Katherine had told her. "John's father has said we cannot be together. He does not want John with this family…and John says he cannot go against his father."

She had cried and cried some more. Selma wanted to comfort her, but what did she know of comforting a girl who had been hurt? No one had taught her that, no one had given her that.

"You must pray, and then try not to think about it," she said. "And I tell you, a father who would say that about us…if you married John that father would always be trouble. You are lucky to get away before."

It didn't seem to help, at least not yet. Katherine had been glad to move, but she was not talking about boys in Grand Rapids except to say, "I won't have nothin' to do with them."

For the boys it was not so bad. Early in summer, when they had first moved to the house in Grand Rapids, the boys came home with bloody noses and torn shirts, but they were holding their own. And already in school they were like back in LaMoure, complaining about the teacher or the homework or the rules, but not so much about what other children were saying.

And some of that was because they were out working, and when Katherine could find work it would help her, too, more than any kind of comforting. "Find some work to do, that will take your mind off it," Mutter had always said. It was true, more true than such things as "you will find other friends."

So Katherine was starting to keep house for a family in town, and Conrad and Fritz, now 15 and 13, were doing farmwork for others, sometimes staying in a hired man's room and not coming home to Selma's house. She hoped the working would not keep them from going to school, but she knew she was losing her hold on that.

"Your father says you must stay in school," she told them over and over, but in her mind she was glad they could work. Every penny they earned counted for something. Even when they worked only for room and board it was something.

The first frost had come this morning, and in the shaded spots the grass was still white, but the day was bright. Selma had milked the cow early, then sent Janey and John, now 11 and 8, to lead the cow to a vacant lot to graze for the day. The children loved the gentle cow, but they hated bringing her home in the evening because she stamped the tether rope all day into her own manure, until the rope was wet and swollen with the green slime.

"Come on, Elizabeth," she said. "You can go with us to the grocery store."

She had Elizabeth lead Lorraine by the hand, while Selma herself and Caroline took turns pulling the little wagon. In it were two wooden boxes with rope handles, in one box two quart jars of cream skimmed from the last two days' milking, and in the other box a gallon of skim milk, both to sell for cash.

They don't like my children and my family, she thought as she walked along. *And they don't like my cow in town. But they like milk and cream, and I like their money.*

One by one, the children got old enough to go alone. By next summer it would be John and Elizabeth taking care of the cow if Janey and Caroline could find work. Each time that happened, there was one less worry in the little day-to-day things, and one less mouth to feed, but that did not make the worrying go away.

It only got...somehow bigger, not easier. They must work so the family stayed together, but working took them away. They must work so they could all stay alive, but even the work children did could be dangerous, or the people they worked for could be dangerous. One could never be sure.

Christina was now 22, married to George Holfer a year, "Georgie" Edith called him and so did the younger children. Nice man. There was hope for them. But even that was a worry, because they were so far away to find work, the Hoover Dam, Georgie doing cement work, which was heavy and dangerous.

But they have a paycheck, Selma thought. *I should be glad for that and worry about nothing else with them.*

Something better than Selma's $35 a month from the county.

More papers. Anything could be done with papers. Tell people in the courthouse that you have eight young children and a husband in jail, and they would give you $35 a month. Like a divorce, it was not so complicated if you could make yourself tell others about your troubles, make yourself forget that you were ashamed and afraid.

Selling cream and milk and eggs was bringing in $10 on a good month.

Rent was $15. They needed to buy hay for the cow, fuel for the winter, underwear for everybody, groceries that could not be raised in the garden.

Clothes they could not buy. Emily and Ludwig were good to send such things from their own children. A few neighbors had been kind enough to give things, too, some of which they had been given themselves from others.

Everybody has not much, Selma thought. The President still said on the radio, "Things will get better," but if that was true it was coming last to North Dakota, and last of that to Selma Wollerman.

So, to the grocery store we go, Selma thought, *with $3.50 to spend.* A little bunch of hobos all in a row, pulling a little wagon, wearing clothes from other people, not very much liked by some along the way. Like some of the hobos that came and went on the freight trains, begging for work…or worse, begging for food. Some people trying to help them, others clubbing them back on the trains.

But we are different than that, too, she thought. *We are in a house. We are living here. The children are in school. I am making their clothes fit, I am sometimes baking for them a cake or a pie, I make a little gift of something for a birthday or Christmas. Katherine does not know it, but I have material to make for her a new dress for school. I take them to church and the oldest take confirmation lessons, perhaps only because I tell them they must do it for their father, but they do it. And they are learning to work. They do not beg.*

We are living here. There are others who have it worse.

Still, many days the shame was so much that Selma wanted only to hide.

"That is Gladys," Elizabeth said, and she waved to a little girl on the porch of a house. The mother came out and pulled the girl inside.

What foolishness, Selma thought. *That woman thinks that means something to me. I am not a child like these little ones. My feelings are not so thin. I will have a friend or two in this town myself.*

Just as the mother shut the door, Selma smiled and waved to her.

I think I go tell her I have a husband, she thought. *My husband is a good farmer, a nice father. You should meet him. Oh, yes, and he killed a man who insulted me. What you think of that?*

But she knew she would never say such a thing. She turned her face away from that house, not wanting that woman to see her face, not able to stop herself.

She looked down at Elizabeth. "Did you bring the soap for her?" she asked, pointing toward the house.

Elizabeth giggled some more.

Two other houses she stopped to deliver cream. Here everything was, "How are you today? Nice to see you, Mrs. Wollerman. Oh, that cream will be so nice. I think we'll be making some ice cream with it. I need some eggs, too, when you have them."

But not, "Come in for coffee, come in and visit."

Still, only three months in town. The day might come.

The grocery store was a worry like everything else. Compared to living out on the farm it was easy. A little walking and here it was. Even in winter it would not be hard. But never enough money to buy much. Especially meat, which she missed from the farm. And always somebody looking at her, looking. Some days she would only send the children, not go to the store herself, staying out of sight in the house.

There had come a day when she knew they would have to leave the Dagel place. Milton Dagel himself had not had to tell her. He had come to visit again and she had told him, once again across the kitchen table with coffee and cookies, nothing fancy because by that time she was lucky to have anything to serve at all.

"I will be leaving in June," she told him in the spring. "My older boys do not want...they cannot keep this farm and their own work, too."

163

It was only a little lie. They could have farmed two places but they argued too much and did not want anything to do with what Otto had had.

And as angry as they made her sometimes, not wanting to farm the place, getting into their own debts and troubles, borrowing grain or horses or the tractor and not paying back, she knew they had to live their own lives, too.

No different than when I left Mutter and my brothers and went off to marry, she thought.

"And I cannot pay enough hired men to do it, so I will let it go," she had told Mr. Dagel.

"You will pay the debts?" he had asked.

"I will pay what I can. Some cows I can sell, and some good horses yet. A little barley and some oats are left."

"What will that leave you?"

"I am not sure," she had answered. "Maybe nothing. We will see."

Almost twelve years they had lived at that place. It was their home, even though Selma had always known it was not their home. Eight children thought of it as home. Otto wrote letters talking of it as home.

But it was too much, and she had known it long before they had moved off. By the time she had paid the debts and moved to Grand Rapids, she had so little left, it was less than when she had left Wilbur Metwald's place over twenty years before.

Fourty-six years old and starting from nothing again.

"Buy some bacon, Ma," Caroline told her. They were standing in front of the refrigerated display case, with ground beef and bacon and roasts all lined up. "And a roast. We could have the roast with mashed potatoes, and some sweet corn."

"That will have to wait," Selma answered. "Maybe later this fall we buy a pig and butcher it ourselves. Then we will have some tasty bacon."

For now it was only another stick of summer-sausage. Thirty-five dollars a month was not enough to buy roasts and bacons, no matter how good they looked.

But, a good sausage was better than nothing.

She had the $3.50 plus another dollar she had made from selling the cream. She spent it all on toiletries, a bag of sugar, and the sausage.

On the way home she had one more stop to make, to deliver the skim milk to Louise Scheffler. Louise was a farm widow, her husband killed by an angry bull. She lived in a narrow, one-bedroom, one-story house with a tiny porch in front. The woman was hard-of-hearing, so everything was a little shouting at her.

Selma knocked on the door hard enough to hurt her knuckles, and got no answer. She waited and knocked again.

"Let's go home," Caroline said. "I have to use the toilet."

"Wait," Selma told her. "We can't leave the milk on the porch. She might not find it before it sours."

She knocked again, and still nothing.

"Watch Lorraine," she told Caroline, and opened the door.

The tiny living room had in it two soft chairs, a little round coffee table, and on the walls rows and rows of small decorative plates hanging. Selma could hear Louise humming and moving around in the next room, the kitchen, so she walked there and said, "Good morning."

Louise didn't appear startled. That was the funny thing. She must have been used to people walking in on her.

"I have brought your milk," she said as loud as she could without shouting.

Louise was taller than Selma, a bony woman with big, gnarled hands.

"Have you brought my milk this morning?" Louise asked.

Selma smiled and nodded.

They went out on the porch and Louise gave Selma $.50 for the milk.

"Thank you," Selma said, looking directly at Louise. Talking went better when Louise could read lips.

"Nice day," Louise said. She looked down at the children, Caroline jigging around where she stood, Elizabeth trying to put Lorraine in the wagon.

"Toilet in the back yard," Louise said to Caroline, pointing and smiling.

Caroline ran around the side of the house.

"Some things cannot wait," Louise said, making both women laugh a little.

They stood saying nothing for a moment, both looking off at the graveled street as a dusty Model-A Ford puttered past, the green ash and elm leaves shimmering in the morning breeze, Elizabeth and Lorraine squalling about the wagon.

"I have some coffee made," Louise said then. "And chocolate-chip cookies. Would you like to sit on the porch with me?"

"Yah, that would be nice," Selma answered quickly, thinking she was shouting.

And it was nice. A nice day. A nice woman this Louise, though talking with her was something of a chore.

Now there would be something good to tell Otto in the next letter.

January 1939

In the afternoon Selma sat down with the little pile of mail. There was another letter from Otto. She did not open it.

This was how people lived without land. And this was how a woman lived without a husband.

Up at 5:00 or 5:30. In winter, stir up the coal fire, start the kitchen stove. Light a lantern and take the chamber pot to the outhouse, go in and wash her hands, back out to milk the cow in her shed in the backyard. Go in and wash up again, get the children up, get them off to school. Spend the day thinking about meals, wondering what to feed them when the money had run out and a few days yet until more was coming. Washing clothes for everybody, scrubbing floors, fixing this, mending that.

When the children were inside, teaching them this, arguing with them about that. Finding places for them to work, trying to keep them safe, punishing them when they refused to learn, getting them to church and confirmation lessons.

Over and over the same.

Once in a while a card or letter from Otto, always nice, but so hard, too. *I wait for him*, Selma thought, *and he is waiting for his freedom.*

Both of us are waiting for something that if it ever comes, will not be what we want of it.

Otto was allowed to send cards that the prison gave out. Each was the same, a square of heavy paper folded in half. On the outside, *A Happy Easter*, or *A Happy Birthday*, and a little pink bow. The print was like the old German script writing, something prisoners learned to pass the time.

Inside, *A token of loving remembrance to mother and family from your loving husband and father, Otto*, he would write. Or *From your husband Otto Wollerman* on Selma's birthday.

It was hard to open these cards and letters. Selma knew that writing letters and getting them, and the few visits Otto had, were for him like a rope thrown short to a drowning man, something that did not save him but kept him from having to say to himself there was no hope. And for Selma, his letters to her were welcome, but the same as for him…a rope thrown too short.

Almost six years he had been gone. Selma had traveled to see him only once or twice a year. It was so far and so expensive, and a bother for anyone who would drive.

This year Lorraine would be 8, Elizabeth 10, John 12, Caroline 14, Janey 15, Fritz 17, Conrad 19, and Katherine 20. All of them six years without a father, six years of too many times eating only noodles and cabbage and a slice of bread with lard, six years of no money and a few times no food at all, six years with a mother watching over them who could not watch everything. Almost six years since that terrifying day when Otto had been wild.

Three years since Mutter had died, her last days very hard for everyone, bedridden for months with no more of her beautiful singing. Janey and Caroline had done much of the work caring for Mutter, and learning then that life and death can go side-by-side in the same house.

This is our life now, Selma thought. *On our own, working at everything that will bring in a penny, or keep from a penny going out. We work and we are living until God ends this world.*

She could not get away from the thing she had heard so much from Mutter and some from the pastors that the End was coming, and like the

Bible said, the troubles and wars and famines they all lived with were a sure sign of it. She tried to tell the children about it, too, so they would not be caught short, sinning when the Lord came. But most days she did not think they were listening.

But right now nobody was dying, and some days they played a little, too. In summer the children took lessons for swimming in the river. In fall and winter the boys trapped muskrats and fox along the river and the sloughs.

Sometimes she and Louise would go to the dances and sit along the side, listening to the music and watching the younger ones whirling and flirting and laughing on the dance floor. Sometimes she and Louise would listen to the radio, Louise with her ear up against the speaker, Selma doing her sewing in a chair nearby. Music came on the radio, but more and more it was talk of Hitler and Germany, and Selma did not like it because the boys were getting to that age.

"You watch about that war," she told the children. "That is from Revelations. It is a sign of the End Times."

Sometimes she would surprise the children with a cake or a new shirt. Once a year they got new shoes, cheap ones, shoes that did not last because they were made of the poorest leather and even cardboard inside, but new anyway.

Always nice to get something new.

She sat there holding Otto's letter, tapping it on the table. It was not the hardest life some have lived, she had told herself over and over. But it was wearing her out. And even if it was a quiet life, more troubles came into it.

She had told Otto once or twice about her headaches, but there was nothing he could do so she had quit that. They had started after he had gone to prison, once a month, though not every month. Migraines, bad enough to put her in bed for two days at a time, the pain beyond what she could tell anyone, and sick to the stomach, too.

She never did tell him about Katherine's troubles, married to a man named Boyd Dahlman. He had pretended to be nice to her when he was in Selma's house, and only Katherine could not see that it was pretending.

"He is a rough talker," Fritz had told his mother. "And he likes to fight in the bars, and he is a mean drinker."

"Say something to your sister," Selma told him. "She will not listen to me."

"I've tried. She don't listen to me either," Fritz answered.

Selma told Otto only that Katherine had been married. It was another of those worries that changed from little day-to-day things, to far away bigger things that showed up in the night, waking Selma and leaving her staring into the darkness.

And John. That boy. The last boy, the one who did not really know a father, just as with Rudy and Daniel years ago. *John is catching the end of my weariness*, she thought. He was rambunctious, always into something. Swimming in the river when it was cold and dangerous, wading in puddles to ruin the new shoes, talking back to the teacher, hanging around the elevator where the men played poker and drank beer.

A beautiful boy, but not easy. And when Selma got a hold of him she was too rough. Spanking him hard, sometimes with Otto's razor strap, so angry that when she started on him she could not stop, but at the same time ashamed of herself.

He will hate me for this, she thought. *I am trying to make him behave but it is not working and he will hate me for it. Soon too big for me to handle, and I am the one who said there should be no beatings in a family. If the end should come when I am doing this, God will send me straight to hell.*

Some days she thought she was going to go mad, especially when the headaches came. She would not be the first woman to do that, would not be the first to send her children away to an orphanage, the first to give up and kill herself.

Such thoughts she tried to keep back. *Find something to do so you don't think about it.* Good words from Mutter. Find something to do to keep the family together.

There was only four left in the house, but still they needed the cow and the chickens and garden and the scratching for everything to stay alive. Janey was working for a farm family for board and room, and she often went to school from there, but still she needed clothes and a little money to spend. Fritz and Conrad worked away, too, both out of school, Katherine gone with Boyd.

That left John, Lorraine, Elizabeth, and Caroline.

John catches the worst of me, Selma thought, *but I am not easy for the girls either. And that is why they are playing away from home whenever they can, and I cannot keep up to them and I do not know what they are doing.*

Almost fifty years old. A grandmother but with four children still to raise, and a husband in jail, and now a husband who says he is not feeling well. Only a hint of it now and again in letters, but another thing to worry about.

The past summer Janey and Fritz had traveled to Bismark with the families they worked for. When they passed the prison, they had seen Otto driving a team in the prison fields, no one else around. They had waved to him, and he back. *He could walk out of there,* Selma had thought when she heard it. *Walk out and come home to help here.*

Foolish thought.

She opened the letter. At the top were the words *Buy Dakota Maid Flour.* She did not understand why that was there, but it was on all the paper Otto was given from the prison.

After that was the prison's orders to whomever used the paper. *Write plainly, no foreign languages, one sheet only,* things like that. Then Otto's words in his handwriting:

To: Selma Wollerman
From: Otto Wollerman
January 22, 1939

Dear Whife and Famely:
recived your welcome letter and was glad to hear from you. I allways fell happy when I get a letter from you. Honey, forgit all the old troubles and forgive me. so when I will some day get home, we will start a new life with lots of sunshine and I will see my old Selma every day.

170

Selma wondered how she could write to him of what was really happening and he could say to forget it. She could not do that, not when the old troubles were what brought on the new troubles, and these she faced every day, and she would ask him what to do but there was nothing he could do, so even with a husband who was not at home she was arguing.

...toward spring when the wether gets warm. you come up here and I have lots of news for you and I will talk things over with you. what is the best to do.

I guess the children like the pincels I sent. what does Conrad and Fritz think about the pens. be shure to bring the boys along when you come up and if Janey comes along I will give her a present. the bread knife I sendt that is for Katerina. I wish her good heldt and good luck the Lord bless her.

With best regards to you and children, in love from your husband and father.

Paul Lenz and Paul Jordan visited me last week.

This time he said nothing about how he was feeling, but the handwriting was changing, shaking a little. Maybe he was giving up. She felt herself choking up and thought she must get busy and do something.

Crying is for nighttime, she told herself, *when you cannot stop it.* But at least the children did not see it then.

Sometimes she cried for Katherine and what could happen to her, sometimes for Anna, married now a long time to that man who ignored her. Sometimes it was for the things John did, and the things she, Selma, did to John. Sometimes she cried for Otto, and sometimes for Selma, too.

Yah, he thinks it will be sunshine someday, she told herself. *I am looking outside at the sunshine right now. But the snow is blowing in it, and the day is so cold, so cold that to go out into it for just a little while is dangerous.*

Sunshine was not everything Otto was thinking it to be.

March 1941

Buy Dakota Maid flour

To: Selma Wollerman
From: Otto Wollerman
March 16, 1941

Darling Selma, I am not well again and the doctor here says it now. yisterday I was to the prole board and the doctor with me. this morning the warden sends me paper that I will be sent home March 31. I am coming into the sunshine, my dear whife, and we will start a new life, now God has blessd us. your husband Otto

Almost eight years he had been gone, and now coming home sick and 60 years old. The world at war, Fritz and Conrad leaving soon for the Navy, and Otto coming home.

Selma did not know what to think of it.

She had waited so long for the time, but always in hope that things would get better, as the President said. And look what came of that. Prices had finally gotten better for grain, but they were no longer farming. And right after that there was war.

Her hands were shaking as she read the letter again. Otto was coming home.

She wanted to call in the children from school, from where Katherine was in Mississippi, from the North Dakota farms the others worked on, to tell them their father would be home, a free man home where he belonged. She wanted to cry with happiness.

And I am happy, she thought. *But the tears are from weariness.*

September 1941

Some things from the past we don't talk about. Some things we get used to. And some things we must fix up, Selma was thinking, sitting in a front pew of the church.

There were two rows of pews with a walk space between, and on the outside ends just enough space for the usher to squeeze along right after a service started and put up on the board the right hymn numbers that should have been there before everyone came in.

The altar was a table covered with a white linen cloth, the Alpha and the Omega on it, beginning and ending. Behind the table was a painting of Christ rising to heaven, the painting so tall it went to the pointed ceiling. A dark, varnished wooden altar rail made a half-circle in front of the table, and the same dark wood continued into thin pillars that held up the painting. On the right side, just at hand level, the varnish was worn off the end of the rail, where hands rested for a moment as rows of people walked through the space behind and came out to drop money in the plates on the left side.

Many times Selma had been in that row of people, shuffling slowly as the line stopped and started, her own hand touching the wooden rail, coming out the other side and dropping in a quarter or two, which seemed to make too much noise, even when they landed on someone else's dollar bills.

She always wished there was a different way of giving an offering, not this little parade up front where everyone left in the pews could see who was giving. When the pastor preached about the widow's mite she thought it was about her, but giving all she had didn't seem to help the feeling of guilt that it was so little.

But today there was no offering and no one to see how much anyone gave. Lorraine and Elizabeth were 11 and 13 and had never been baptized, and Otto had agreed they must have this done. So there in the church was the family all dressed up in the best hand-me-downs they owned, and there was the pastor reading the service from the hymn book:

"Hear the Holy Gospel, which saith: they brought young children to him that he should touch them; and his disciples rebuked those that brought them. But when Jesus saw it, he was much displeased, and said unto them, 'Suffer the little children to come unto me, and forbid them not, for of such is the kingdom of God. Verily I say unto you, whosoever shall not receive the kingdom of God as a little child, he shall not enter

therein...'"

Getting the girls baptized was a relief from the burden of those words. Half-grown already they were, in new black shoes, blue sweaters, and white dresses that Janey and Caroline had both worn, and which Selma had re-fit by hand. *They look so innocent,* Selma thought, *and the innocent ones should live in heaven even if they have not been baptized.* But the Word was the Word, and she was not willing to question it aloud. So many dangers in growing up, and if they had not lived, and were not baptized, the message was clear. They would not have gone to heaven. But now at least that one danger was past.

Otto had seemed surprised when Selma had told him about the girls.

"Why were they not baptized?" he asked her.

"You were not so much for the church in those years," she reminded him.

Otto himself had gone to see the pastor about it. That was one of the things different now…a husband who took care of family business. She liked it, but she was not used to it.

Since the girls were not of an age to answer for themselves, Selma and Otto had to stand and answer for them. Selma wished she had a new dress, but she had only the old blue one with the lace collar and short sleeves, and a small black hat just as old.

But clean and not frayed, she thought.

Otto was in the same suit he had worn in front of the judge in 1933. It had hung in the house all the time, and he had put on no weight, so they had brushed it up and bought him a new white shirt.

"Since in Christian love you present these children for Holy Baptism, I charge you that you diligently and faithfully teach them the Ten Commandments, the Creed, and the Lord's Prayer…"

Selma thought at least that they…she…had done.

"I therefore call upon you to answer in their stead: Do you renounce the devil, and all his works, and all his ways?"

"I renounce them," Selma and Otto said together.

It was strange to be standing here, looking like a family, so strange that Selma thought it was like she was watching it from the outside, but still within it herself. She had had the feeling many times since Otto came home.

Otto was right. They were in the sunshine of life, starting new. But it was confusing…as if the years since he had gone away had never happened, but at the same time those years were Selma's real life, and this new one was something she was just watching others live in.

"Do you present these children to be baptized into this Christian faith?"

"I do."

"Let us pray."

Starting a new life. Otto was working here and there, fixing up things for people, hauling garbage, anything for a few dollars. And every dollar made things a little easier.

And people liked him. A few still turned up their noses, but very few. He was such a good talker, such a good man to work, the rest said.

But it could not be the new life he had in his mind, and that she did not tell him. He could never start farming all over again, never build a dairy, never have land to pass on to his children. He could not ignore that he was not so strong anymore, that his hands shook, that he had headaches and weak spells when he must stay in bed for the day.

And he could not ignore that his years in prison and the shame that his children had pushed to the back of their minds, had become for them the only life they knew. They could not now pretend nothing had been wrong, could not so quickly start a new life with a real father.

One at a time, the girls leaned over the baptismal font. The pastor read: *"Lorraine Wollerman, I baptize thee in the name of the Father, and of the Son, and of the Holy Ghost, Amen. Elizabeth Wollerman, I baptize…"* touching the water to the girls' foreheads three times, and handing each a clean handkerchief to dry themselves.

It was a Sunday afternoon, and as they left the church Otto was beaming. "I am making ice cream for everybody," he said. "To celebrate. And I want to walk uptown with the girls, so the whole town can see them in their white dresses."

"Pa," Elizabeth said. "Let's take the car."

"Today we walk. Just for a little while," he answered. "You should be proud that people see you this way."

And it was a celebration for the rest of the day. With Janey helping, Selma cooked a big supper with a real ham she had put in earlier in the day. Louise brought a pie and a little book of prayers for the girls. Otto had for the girls each a tiny pin—a golden cross—to remember the day.

Later in the evening company came, Mr. and Mrs. Strauss for a few minutes to congratulate the girls. "Soon they will begin confirmation lessons," Otto told them. "So grown up they are getting."

And more company, though probably not for Lorraine and Elizabeth. Charles Knickerbocker, Janey's boyfriend, some years older and a worry for Selma, but a man who was polite and known to be a worker, a man who wanted to fly airplanes for the Army Air Corps.

When Charles and Otto visited, they spoke mostly to each other. Charles was smart with machines, and Otto liked to hear about them, though he knew he had fallen behind when he was gone to prison. Once they started it didn't bother Otto that Charles spoke only English.

"Tell me about this hay baler machine," he told Charles this evening. "I have seen the bales, and I was thinking how fast the haying would go with that, but I don't know how it works."

"Pretty simple, really," Charles said. "It's got a roller with steel fingers that pick up the windrow…well, you know there's two kinds. The older ones you bring the hay to it, but now they've got 'em with a motor mounted right on the baler, so you pull it right down the windrow with a tractor or a team."

"It picks up the windrow like the loader we pull behind the hay wagons?"

"Same thing, only it works even better because it's rolling under the windrow instead of on top of it."

"Yah, that makes sense. It's in front, not behind."

"Right. Then that big flywheel drives a plunger," Charles told him, his hands and arms talking like his voice, "which rams the hay into the square chute, and a shear drives off the flywheel, too, and it cuts off the hay coming in from the rollers, so that shapes it into a bale."

"And tying off the wire, that is for the man who rides there?"

"Yes, but now they're coming out with twine balers, and they've got a knotter just like the old grain binders, so they don't need anybody riding on them."

Even John was quiet listening to that. He seemed to be happy just sitting there with the men, not trying to go off somewhere by himself.

Janey helped with the dishes, since Charles was talking with Otto. *Otto should quit talking,* Selma thought, *so Janey and Charles can go out for a walk together...but then if they are inside I don't have to worry about them.*

As it got dark outside Selma lit the kerosene lamps and moved about the house, picking up a bit of wrapping paper, some empty coffee cups, some crumbs from the desserts. After a while she sat in her rocking chair. It was still early but she was getting sleepy, and her mind drifted watching the family.

This is what our life should be, she was thinking. *Good things are happening. We are not starving. At night Otto calls me sweetheart and holds onto me...* Sometimes he held her so much that he was more like a child than a husband, and still asking for forgiveness. But this was a new life, and it was fine.

Still, so much had happened before it that she could not be at ease. *It is like baking a cake,* she thought, a sweet thing everybody wanted. The world had not ended yet. But all it took to make it fall was somebody to slam the oven door too hard.

She watched the family talking some more, faces brightening and fading as they passed in and out of the lamplight, laughter coming easily from them. The windows were black now. Outside there was war coming, and old troubles still alive and new ones being born. Inside everybody was happy and safe.

I should pull down the shades, Selma thought.

Chapter

Ten

Reunion, 1982: Day Three

"We should have been told this years ago, when we were kids," one of the third generation said. "Why were you all dodging this?"

That question was getting repetitious.

"A lot of it we were ashamed of," one of the seconds finally replied. "We just pushed it back all the time when we were young, and it kind of stayed that way."

"Why? Why? My God, it wasn't something you did. It wasn't even something to be ashamed of. You should have just told those people…the ones with their noses in the air…to shove it. I bet they had some skeletons in their closets, too."

Even more pointed questions began. "What's the real reason he got out so early? Fifteen to twenty-five years, and he serves…what…eight years? Somethin' hinky there, even if he was sick."

"That's easy," the answer came, also within the third generation. "Maybe the state figures he's gonna die, so why spend any medical bills on him? Send him home. Let the family pay. Or the county. Whomever."

"You don't think it was a parole board feeling sorry for him, like the judge and prosecutor that sent him up? Or time off for good behavior?"

"Nah. Jails weren't crowded then like now. And they were getting labor out of him right up till he left. I doubt there was anything humanitarian going on. Plus, you got to figure, that sentence he had, people weren't into bleeding-heart rehab programs and halfway houses and all that. 'You do the crime, you do the time' was their attitude. I'm betting it was cost, nothin' else."

One of Lorraine's daughters had a question she sent up the ladder to Selma. "What were the two of you arguing about by letter?"

No answer came back down.

But even though the generation gap stopped some of the queries, the questions drew out a lot of side stories, too, like those from Conrad.

"Me and Fritz went up to Fargo to enlist," he told one group. "Didn't have a damned dime between us, so we rode a freight train, sneaked up on top. Signed the papers, jumped another freight for home. This time we got caught. Engineer was going to pitch us off but he asked what the hell we thought we were doing, so we told him. Changed him completely. He said, 'You boys are riding up front with me,' and that's what we did."

And another group talking about farm life got more of his stories. "Me and Fritz used to take fresh cow...you know, and fill up a bucket with it. You let that stand out in the sun and wind for about a week and it dried so hard you could tap around the edges and take the whole thing out and sit on it. Made a great stool."

"And a whole new angle on the word 'stool,'" one of his listeners said, laughing.

"Yeah, but the best part was this. You leave it dry only a couple of days and you could still tap it out of there. But it was plum soft inside yet. Those we saved for the neighbor kids, especially if their parents brought them over all dressed up." He roared with laughter, leaning back and slapping his knee. "We'd say, 'Here, you take this one,' and plop, down they'd go. What a mess."

Besides the stories there were long discussions about time and forgotten faces. "That was in '41" would bring "No, that was '38," which would be answered with "No, '41, because their barn burned the same year that happened, and the fire was '41," which was rebutted

179

with "Ain't that the barn that burned twice and the neighbors said it was for insurance? If it was '41, that was the second time, so I'm right."

Inevitably, talk came around to the way Grandma had dealt with the kids' behavior once Otto was gone. When that subject came up, the generation gap became clearer, and the talk began to tiptoe around things that obviously hadn't been forgotten.

"I remember Grandma's brother, Uncle Ludwig, visiting us," John mentioned. "He always wore a black suit when he left the farm. Like he was traveling to New York City for cryin' out loud. And a black…what did they call 'em…bowler hat? I remember thinking if he had a gun he'd be Wyatt Earp."

"But he was nice to us kids," Caroline told him. "And so was Uncle Henry."

"Yeah, felt sorry, I guess."

"And Aunt Emily, she was a gem."

"Had a better life than Ma did, that's why."

"Well, maybe Emily was warpin' on her kids, too, when things were bad. You never know."

"Were things really that bad? Bad enough to send Ma over the edge like she was sometimes?"

"I don't know. She had her reasons, I guess."

"That didn't make it feel any better when that razor strap landed."

"But she must have…I don't know. Look at her now. She isn't that kind of person. We didn't know what she was living with, I guess. We just thought this is what life is."

"That still don't make it right, and don't mean it's forgotten."

"It wasn't like that after Pa came home, you know."

"Maybe, maybe not. I wasn't around long enough to find out."

"We all took off pretty early."

"Not like now, kids hanging around till they're 30."

"Raising kids is never easy," one of the third generation popped up. "I've got three and sometimes it's more than I can handle. You know that. You've all had kids. And you've had your hard times. But you also had a decent paycheck all the time. Grandma had no money, no help. Add it up."

"Still don't make it right," a voice repeated.

"I suppose not," the answer came back, "but it wasn't reason enough to shut off the next generation from everything, either. Nobody is saying they were saints. We're just saying these were people to remember, not people to forget. And there was so much history that we could have learned…family history and just, you know, regular history…but now we're all scattered and it's too hard to pull it together. That's where you did us wrong."

But by late in the third day, some folks already heading for their scattered homes, all the stories, the arguments, the generation gap, had begun to melt together. It was all just one story, and they were all talking as if they were part of it.

Chapter Eleven

March 20, 1942

Selma could hear the pastor's voice but she was not thinking of his words.

Janey had been the one to see Otto go down.

She had been leaving the outhouse in the back yard, watching her footing on the frozen path, barely daylight, the January day bitter cold. When she looked up, there was her father coming toward her, and at that moment he had fallen to the ground.

"Ma! Ma! Pa needs help!" were the words from Janey's face stuck quickly in the back door, the first that Selma knew. Selma had run outdoors still with slippers on her feet and shook Otto, but he did not respond.

They tried to lift him but couldn't until John came to help.

Selma couldn't get rid of the picture in her mind, a man lying on his back in the snow, arms moving a little, face with no color, mouth open and eyes, too, as if surprised, but unable to speak, unable to...

She did not know if he had heard them shouting and asking him questions.

After that Selma felt only numb for days. There had been too many changes, too much hope, and now so quickly back to what the family had been before Otto came home.

A proud man's life came to this...a stroke on his way to the outhouse. Two months bedridden, women feeding him bread softened in broth, carefully pulling aside his cheeks and looking inside for pieces that might collect in the paralyzed jaws and choke him when no one was with him. Women bathing him, cleaning up after his bowel movements. Nothing left of his strength. A helpless, bony old man...not even a man, if he could have been asked about it.

I am living my mother's life, Selma thought.

There would be no more of starting over with a new life, a father for the children's few more years of growing up, a few extra dollars coming in, a husband taking care of family business.

But this time she knew what life would be. She had been living it before he came home, and she told herself she could do it again if she must.

She knew she should be weeping at the funeral, but caring for Otto since the stroke had left her feeling that she knew what was coming, knew it would be a relief for him and for her, too. *I will be crying again when no one sees*, she thought. *But not today.*

"*Lord, now lettest thou servant depart in peace, according to thy word*," the pastor read. "*For mine eyes have seen thy salvation which thou has prepared before the face of all people; A light to lighten the Gentiles, and the glory of thy people Israel.*"

It was good that Otto was in the church now. He would go to heaven where he would be in peace for his sins.

And it was good to see that so many came for his funeral. All the children that could be there, and the Retzlaffs from Kulm, neighbors and old friends from Edgeley, some from Grand Rapids. Selma wondered if they had all forgotten, or forgiven, or what their thoughts would be at the funeral of a man such as Otto.

She listened more closely as the pastor read Otto's obituary:

"Karl Otto Wollerman, 60, a Grand Rapids resident for the last year, died Tuesday, march 17, 1942, at 2:15 a.m. of a cerebral

hemorrhage.

He was stricken ill on Jan. 9 and had been bedridden since then.

Mr. Wollerman was born at Hammerstein, West Prussia, Aug. 22, 1881, and came to America as a young man, locating in LaMoure county where he was engaged in farming.

He was especially noted for his excellent care of horses, having had special training for this while in Germany.

He married Ruth Schloven in 1913. She died in 1918.

On April 22, 1919, he married Mrs. Selma Retzlaff Metwald. To this union 8 children were born.

He leaves his widow, eight daughters, and five sons.

Pallbearers were Harry Junod, Lee Stewart, Richard Gussman, R.A. Holen, L.E. Johnson, and Frank Dathe.

Funeral services Friday, March 20, in the Zion Lutheran Church."

Selma thought that something more than that should have been written for him. Something about a man who could jump so lightly onto a tall horse and ride 30 miles on a winter day; a smart man, curious, who roamed the countryside studying cattle and land to make better his farming; a man with dreams to be something, yet who did more working than dreaming; a man who saw those dreams falling away piece-by-piece; a man with a quick temper, yet kinder to children than his wife could be; a man who took into his life an abandoned woman and called her "darling" and made for her a good life, who took into his life other men's children and tried to love them, too; a man too proud to let an insult be said; a man taken to slavery by drink; a man who begged forgiveness from the woman he had hurt.

No, she decided, *it is written the way it should be. Short. Plain.* All the rest was too sad…much too complicated. No one would ever understand.

It was best not to talk about these other things, and Selma made up her mind that she would not think about them, would not ever talk about them.

All that would be buried with Otto.

November 15, 1944

LaMoure Chronicle, November 15, 1944:

Fritz Wollerman, Naval gunner's mate, son of Mrs. Selma Wollerman, has been killed in action, according to word received by Mrs. Wollerman from the U.S. Navy Dep't, as noted in this week's Grand Rapids news.

Joint Memorial Services for the late Fritz Wollerman, 23, and S/Sgt Ashley Hennings, 28, both of whom were killed in the South Pacific, were conducted at Zion Lutheran Church at Grand Rapids on Sunday afternoon. Many memorial gifts were given by relatives, friends, and both families.

Fred August (Fritz) Wollerman, son of Carl Otto Wollerman and his wife Selma, was born December 30, 1921. He was brought to the Lord and Savior in the sacrament of Holy Baptism on the 17th of February, 1928.

The baptismal vows were renewed by him in the holy rite of confirmation in the Zion Lutheran Church in Grand Rapids on May 24, 1936.

He attended Grand Rapids public schools through the 10th grade. He joined the Navy on July 16th, 1940, and received his training at the Great Lakes Naval Training Station and was assigned to duty on the USS Mississippi for some time. He was changed to another ship, the USS Birmingham, which went down in rescue efforts of the USS Princeton. It was during this action that Wollerman died.

The four years he spent serving his country took him to many parts of the globe.

He is preceded in death by his father, who died March 18, 1942, and is survived by his mother, Mrs. Selma Wollerman of Grand Rapids and four brothers and seven sisters. He reached the age of 22 years, 9 months, and 24 days.

Everyone was so sure that dying for the country was a brave thing.

Selma did not know if she could agree with that when it was your own son. What she did know was that she had seen more deaths than she could bear.

Little Martha, then Vater, then little August Wollerman and Ruth Wollerman, then Mutter and Otto and now Fritz.

They all are leaving me behind, she thought, *leaving me in this life, which some days seems nothing more than loneliness and weariness. So many leaving that I am no longer feeling anything when it happens. No wonder Mutter sang over and over about the welcome rest that comes with death.*

But I am still here, and I can work, and I will live until I die. Complaining makes no help and is a weakness that others can see.

Chapter Twelve

Saturday, August 11, 1963

Living in a basement had its ups and downs. It was so dark in winter that without electric lights it would be unbearable, no better than the sod hut from Selma's childhood. But in summer a basement stayed cool on the hottest days, not too bad even if you were cooking all day.

She got up at 6:00 and started setting out jars for canning. Elizabeth's husband and kids had brought over a dozen walleyed pike the night before, all cleaned, most of them two pounds, a couple bigger.

Selma had stuck them in buckets with ice water, and when she pulled them out this morning she scrubbed them again before cutting them in chunks crosswise. Several pieces could be stuffed in each quart jar, along with a dash of salt and a bit of vegetable oil.

When she had all the fish prepared, she put the jars in the pressure cooker and looked at the time. It was almost 7:00. Fish took 90 minutes, so while that was going she could get started on some dill pickles. They were easy. Slice up the cucumbers into a jar, put in some dill and a bit of red pepper. Harvey and his boys always brought more fish than the family could eat, so some would be given away, and whoever took it might like some pickles, too.

She hummed as she worked. Some of it was in no tune at all, some of it old hymns. *I have become my mother,* she thought, *except Mutter had a beautiful voice.*

Between humming the songs she went through in her mind a list of people, her children and others, a habit she had started after the death of Fritz, as if each day she had to make a check of all of them to see if they were still alive. After a while she ate a bowl of cold cereal. So easy now…milk from the store, keep it in the refrigerator. She had not made up her bed yet so that was next, down the little hallway past the tiny bathroom, past the oval picture of Otto on parade on that military horse.

A lifetime away that was, she thought each time she looked at it. *A lifetime away. I am…74, so he would have been…82, this year.*

And what if he had lived? What would life be?

She could not picture that. She simply looked at the picture and remembered him as he had been, and of all the memories the best was like this picture, when on a cold March day he had ridden into her life so sure of himself.

After she had made the bed she climbed the steps to the entrance and went out into the sunshine. She had four rows of sweet corn, and she went down the rows gently pulling the husks open an inch or two at the top, her thumbs pushing aside the strands of cornsilk.

She thought that the corn would be ready for canning by Monday.

And for eating, too, though very carefully so that she didn't leave her false teeth stuck in a cob.

Next she went down the two rows of string beans, her quick hands pushing aside the leaves, dropping the beans into a small bucket. *These are done,* she thought. The last picking. Next week would be these beans and some corn, some peppers, and more pickles to can, and maybe more fish.

Across the alley from her garden she saw Mrs. Stanford setting her three cats out the door. Selma waved and so did Mrs. Stanford. Nice lady, good neighbor, but her house smelled of cats.

Sometimes when she visited Gladys Stanford, Selma thought of the time in Grand Rapids when a little girl named Gladys had a mother who said hurtful things. It had seemed so important then. It seemed so unimportant now.

This Gladys was such a nice lady except for the one annoying thing she asked every time. "When is Rudy going to finish the house?"

Rudy and his wife Rebecca traveled the whole country working. Someday they would come home to LaMoure and put a house on top of the basement, but Selma had no idea when. She had told that to Gladys at least fifty times, but Gladys must have been bothered by it, looking out her kitchen window, seeing that flat roof just above the ground across the alley, and every so often an old woman popping up out of it like a striped gopher on the prairie.

Selma had long ago decided that Gladys could think what she wanted. That basement was cool in summer, warm in winter. It had running water and electricity and a good oil stove. Even a toilet. No more trips to the outhouse.

Though a bathtub would have been nice.

By the time Selma had finished picking and washing the beans, the fish were ready. She turned off the stove and went to brush her hair and do a little sponge bath. She was going to stop at Elizabeth's house before she went uptown for some cinnamon and a pound of butter.

It was getting close to 10:00 by the time she had walked the few blocks to Elizabeth's.

"Grandma, you're up already," Harvey said when he came to the screen door.

It was his joke always.

"I thought I would come over and wake you," she said back.

They sat at the kitchen table with coffee and waited for the orange rolls Elizabeth had in the oven.

"Lorraine and Edward are coming after a while, but we can start on these now," Elizabeth said.

"Say, Grandma, did you hear about Ole and Lena?" Harvey asked.

"I think I don't want to hear it."

"Yeah, they finally got married, you know. And Lena had six kids in seven years. So she and her friend Borghild were talking, and Lena says, 'Yah, I'm pregnant again. It's a good ting I got married you know. I was chock full of the little buggers.'"

189

Harvey laughed and laughed. He was the only Norwegian married into the family.

"Norwegians," Selma told him.

He was a handsome man, slim, quick-moving, working long hours at his job in an office.

"I want to hear about your visit up to Janey's," Elizabeth said.

"She is fine, just fine," Selma answered. "They are going to add on to the house, a big living room. And her Karen has a boyfriend now."

"Really?"

"Yah, a Norwegian. Too bad."

"Very funny, Grandma," Harvey growled at her.

"A farm boy?" Elizabeth asked.

"Well, he comes from farm families, but his father is a teacher with Charles. The boy goes to college. I think he is too old for Karen, but…" she shrugged her shoulders, "…the age is not everything."

"Karen is a smart girl. And Charles is a scary father."

"The boy needs some scaring," Selma answered. "He brags too much. And thinks he is a cowboy."

"A Minnesota cowboy?" Harvey smiled. "What does he round up? Mosquitoes?"

"I canned the fish this morning," Selma said. "You want some of it back?"

"Nah," Harvey replied. "There'll be more. The kids want to go again this evening."

"I'll give some to Gladys then. Her Clifford likes fish. And keep some for later."

"Maybe take some to Conrad when you go," Delores said.

"Yah, a suitcase full of fish all the way to California?"

Elizabeth laughed. "No, Ma. I mean one or two jars. So he gets a taste of North Dakota walleyes."

"We will see," Selma answered. "I think they have fish in California, too."

She finished her coffee before she spoke again. "Conrad says we go to the Knott's Berry Farm. What is that?"

"Oh, they grow all kinds of stuff…flowers, vegetables, everything for warm climates. Well, that's what I've read. We've never been there," Elizabeth answered, looking over at Harvey. "Maybe some day."

"Well, that I will like. The bus ride…it gets long. But still it is fun, if you get somebody good to sit with."

"I worry about you on your trips," Elizabeth said.

"I am fine. Nobody bothers an old lady."

"If they do, she can clobber them with a jar of canned fish," Harvey said.

Always the jokes with him.

"I must get busy," she said then.

"Stick around," Harvey said. "We can watch some baseball on the TV."

"Hmph," Selma snorted. "I cannot waste my day with that. I have to bake for church tomorrow."

When she got home from the store Selma made a sandwich with lettuce, a bit of cheese, some summer sausage. She ate that while sitting in her rocking chair and listening to the news on the radio. Something about Castro and Cuba, which she knew nothing about except she remembered Vater complaining about the Americans being in a war over there long ago. Some things changed so much, but other things didn't change at all.

When Fritz had been killed the Navy had offered his insurance as a choice to Selma: a one-time payment of $5,000, or monthly payments of $75 for the rest of her life. She had decided that if she had it all, it would disappear.

So she had that monthly payment and a little life insurance that Otto had put on her long ago, without her knowing. She had no rent to pay, at least until Rudy and Rebecca finished the house. She had a bit of Social Security, and her children sent her bus tickets to come and visit, and sometimes her brother Henry, long divorced, came to stay a while in the other bedroom and helped with the groceries, and so it seemed she always had enough money.

In fact, though she told no one except Elizabeth and Lorraine, she had a savings account. Such a change from the early part of her life, when extra money was something she had no hope for.

In winter she sat in her basement crocheting rugs by the dozen for gifts or charity. Some evenings she went over to Gladys' house and some other friends came and they all played pinochle and drank coffee.

And sometimes she traveled. She loved getting on the Greyhound and watching the miles blur past the windows, towns and mountains and deserts, farms and cattle and forests, going and going to places she had barely even heard of when she was young. She had been to Texas to help Christina with her family. New Mexico, Washington, California, Wyoming, Minnesota.

And the roads so good, she always thought. Nothing like a trip with Kurtzie and Schnauze and a wagon with no springs on miles of frozen ruts.

One place she would like to go again now because it would be so much nicer was Washington, where Katherine lived and her husband Boyd who had died this summer, and none too soon because everyone in the family was afraid he would somehow destroy Katherine before he was gone.

How that had happened was beyond understanding. Why Katherine had not run away...

She could not have run away. She was trying to mother four children, and that Boyd Dahlman was so mean he would have hunted her down anyway.

Selma felt guilty thinking that death was not always hard to take. Boyd's death had made her happy.

It was so hard to think about a daughter's life being that terrible, but now it was past. Little Katherine, no bigger than Selma herself, beaten and frightened, and her children, too, yet Katherine had raised them and cooked for them all and kept a clean house and planted flowers and kept the children in school, and never called for help. Only a little now and then on the telephone she told her sisters and brothers, so the family knew how bad it was.

I was strong, Selma thought. *I had terrible things happen. But I had Mutter and my brothers Ludwig and Henry, and for a time, a wonderful husband Otto.*

Much of the time Katherine had had no one. But maybe now that terrible thing could heal.

On the kitchen table she set out ingredients for a banana-cream pie and cinnamon rolls. She didn't need written recipes for something as simple as this. She put the pie in the oven first, and while it was baking she cleaned up the sink and counter from the canning she had done in the morning.

It was enjoyable to cook this way, an electric range, grocery store a few minutes away, no hurry, money for all the right ingredients, and tomorrow for the potluck meal people would be saying, "Where's Selma's cooking? Leave some of Selma's stuff for me."

So easy compared to her years of growing up. And so…bountiful, compared to the years in Grand Rapids when the children would come home starving from swimming lessons and she had nothing to give them but a slice of bread with lard on it.

Sometimes she wondered if this was the life Otto wanted for them…peaceful and plentiful, with a few friends and time to watch the grandchildren grow.

But Otto had not been able to make it happen. *Maybe God made it happen,* she thought. If that was what it was, then He must have forgiven the times she had been too rough with the children, the times she had wondered if God cared at all about her life, the times she had sinned with Otto in his bed, the times she had wished punishment on Wilbur Metwald.

Otto should have been alive to share this life.

Sometimes she was lonely without him, yet sometimes it was good not to be worrying about a man at all.

With the smell of baking cinnamon rolls filling the kitchen Selma sat down for a little while in her rocking chair. Her crocheting was alongside and she picked up where she had left off the day before on it, her fingers flying in the yarn. She did not need to turn on a light yet. Plenty of light came in through the window-wells in the summer.

At quiet times like this her mind wanted to go back to the troubles that had been her life for so long, and to the man who had for a little while made her happy. She had to keep herself thinking about other things, keep her hands busy, so that the other life would stay hidden away.

It's best not to talk about it, she told herself again and again. *Do something to take your mind off it.*

The late afternoon sun beamed straight onto her work from the tiny window. *Someday*, she thought, *I will live with bigger windows.*

She wondered if Otto was in the sunshine now.

Chapter Thirteen

Reunion: Bigfork, Montana: 1982

It was the third day and almost everyone was getting ready to leave. There had been swimming and boat rides and fishing, lots of getting acquainted with strangers of the same blood, more tables weighted with food lovingly prepared by generations of good cooks, and in the midst of it all, everybody talking about Selma and Otto.

Selma herself was worn out but happy.

Different ones had come and gone as she talked to them. Only a few had listened to it all, some of her own children, that was what was important, and a few from the next generation. But it was enough. The rest could hear it from them.

"I did all of this," Selma said again as she watched people pack their cars and say their good-byes.

And they were good people, people who didn't let a little suffering get them down, people who never asked for a handout, people who mowed their lawns and planted flowers, people who taught their daughters to cook and clean and their sons to work and both to fear God, though maybe not enough sometimes because there was still swearing when they thought Grandma couldn't hear them.

Otto would have been proud of them, she thought. Angry at some things, but those things passed, and they were good people still. She wished Otto could know, and she wished Fritz could have been here, too.

One thing Otto would have thought was strange, though. Almost none of them were farmers.

There were teachers and housewives, nurses and bookkeepers, policemen and store owners and firefighters.

But especially in the third generation, almost no farmers, and the few were on farms they had from the family. In fact, as far as Selma knew, none of the rest owned any land at all, maybe an acre or two with a house on it. *How did that happen?* she wondered. *How could all these people live without land?*

"Do you know what you have said, Ma?" asked Janey, who was starting another pot of coffee and finishing the breakfast dishes, and at the same time simmering stew meat that would be in the soup at lunchtime, and at the same time telling her daughters to pick up this and put away that. Elizabeth and Lorraine, Catherine and Caroline, were all still at the table, but staying out of the way. It was Janey's kitchen, after all.

Selma was drying the bowls and stacking them on the counter. "I told them about your father," she answered. "We had so much troubles, but he was a good man. They should know that."

"Yes, I guess that's good," Janey said. "But it's more about you than about Pa."

"What is it of me?" Selma said snappishly. "I did nothing but what I had to. Your father should not be forgotten, and no one should be ashamed of him. That is what had to be said."

Janey took the bowl from Selma's hands and stopped the towel for a moment, looking at Selma. "And that's fine, but don't you realize what you yourself did? Even us kids that knew Pa, we were thinking about our own growing up and our own lives. We weren't thinking about you. And later when we wanted to know more about Pa and you wouldn't talk about it, we still weren't thinking of you. It was about him. But you...you held it all together."

"I just worked," Selma said, and took the bowl back from Janey. "It was what I knew to do. And sometimes I was too rough, and sometimes we had friends to play cards with and visit, so then it wasn't so bad."

"Ma, you're incredible," Caroline said between the last bites of her cinnamon roll. "I was too young to understand much, except for the kids being nasty to us in school. But I agree with Janey. It's more about you than about Pa."

"Don't you say that," Selma said quickly. "You should not forget him. He was a good man."

These girls, good girls, but always wanting to argue, she thought.

"Well, I'm glad to hear he was a good man," Elizabeth said. "Because I had just blotted it all out. I just wish you hadn't waited so long to say it."

"Ya, that was wrong," Selma said, nodding her head and feeling saddened. She stood with the dishtowel, motionless. "But you were so young and we had so much to do. And then the war came, and we lost Fritz…"

She laid the towel on the counter. "I think I will sit down now," she said. "Lorraine, you finish drying these dishes. I want a little coffee."

She could hear the girls talking about her while they finished the dishes.

"I was just tired of living with her by that time," one of them said. "I couldn't think of anything but getting away, but when I finally did, that wasn't so hot either, not at first anyway."

"It's hard to think of her as being…you know…in love. I'm sure I saw some of it when we were still all together on the farm, but those later years it just…I don't know. There wasn't much room for anything like that when we were about half-starved and Pa was gone anyway."

It was always that way with an old person in the house…people talking as if the old person couldn't hear. But Selma didn't mind. She had other things to think about.

She was going to drive back to North Dakota with Lorraine and Jack, starting in the morning. A long trip, but nice. Maybe now she could just sit and watch the miles go by. Maybe now when she got home she would not always have to tell herself, 'Get busy and do something so you don't think about it.' She was too old to be busy anyway, and that she knew. It seemed like a whole day could go by and she got nothing done at all.

"Janey," she said, interrupting their talk. "The pictures and the letters, these must go on to the grandchildren now."

"Which grandchildren? You mean just my girls?"

"No, no. Any that want them. You girls decide, but they must be sure to take care of them."

Selma thought again about the long trip home, hours and hours across the prairies. Travel was a kind of waiting all its own, waiting to get someplace, waiting to get home, but a nice kind of waiting. Not hurtful like waiting for Otto had been.

Maybe Otto was waiting for her now.

Maybe she could finish crocheting a little rug on the way home. She hoped the neighbors had remembered to water her flowers while she was gone.

LaMoure, North Dakota: 1990
From the Fargo, North Dakota *Forum*, June 23, 1990

Entered into eternal rest: Tuesday, June 19, 1990: Selma Wollerman:

The funeral for Selma Wollerman, 101, LaMoure, ND, will be at 10:30 Saturday in Zoar Lutheran Church, LaMoure. Visitation will be from 1 to 9 today, with a prayer service at 8, in Dahlstrom Funeral Home, LaMoure. She died Tuesday.

Selma Retzlaff was born May 28, 1889, in Russia. In 1892, she moved with her family to the Kulm, ND area. She married Wilbur Metwald in 1907. He preceded her in death.

She married Otto Wollerman, April 22, 1919, in Edgeley, ND. They farmed near LaMoure. In 1932 they moved to the Grand Rapids, ND area, where they farmed. He died in 1942. She moved to LaMoure in 1947, and in 1987 she became a resident of LaMoure Healthcare Manor.

She is survived by three sons and seven daughters, 40 grandchildren, 84 great grandchildren, and 18 great-great grandchildren.

In a back pew at Selma's funeral, one of the great grandaughters stopped chewing her gum long enough to point to the obituary and whisper to her cousin, "She lived like...a hundred and one years, and this is it?"

"Yeah," the other whispered back.

"What did she do all that time, besides having like...fifty babies."

The other shrugged her shoulders. "Nothin', I guess," she whispered. "I mean, women weren't allowed to do anything, so..."

The first one whispered again, "I remember her from that time we all went to Montana, to that reunion? She was all...pudgy, and wrinkled. Everybody was talking about something she said, but I didn't understand. So this was like...her whole life. A hundred and one years—not even a career, never allowed to find her true self."

She leaned toward her cousin. "I'm glad we don't have to live like her," she whispered. "I mean, her life was like totally meaningless. Her self-esteem must have been super low."

She sat back for a moment and popped her gum, then leaned over and whispered some more. "Next week I'm getting my own car. Lance is going to be just wired when he sees it."

"Cool," the second girl replied. "Are you taking it to Bismarck?"

"Nooo," the first said, pouting. "My dad says not the first semester, till he sees what my grades are."

"Bummer. My dad's the same way."

The service dragged on, the pastor and other speakers repeating each other with words such as "hardship," "struggle," "role model," and "resilience."

"What are they talking about?" the first girl whispered toward the end of it. "I don't get it."

"Me either," came the reply. "I can't picture her being...you know...alive. And young. And it's not like we're connected."

They fidgeted away the rest of the service—short, strong, dark-haired, dark-eyed late-teens with tiny waists and smooth skin, waiting to get on with their own lives.

A fterword

Waiting for Otto is a work of fiction.

The two main characters' names, as well as some events and some locations, are drawn from an actual family's sketchy written and oral history. However, characters' thoughts and feelings, the fabric of characters' interrelationships, many names, all dialogue, details of setting, and many characters are products of the author's imagination.

That said, the verifiable elements are these:

Selma Retzlaff was born in Bessarabia in 1889, and migrated to Kulm, North Dakota, with her parents in 1891, where they all lived in a sod house for some time. On that home farm Selma lost her younger sister Martha to a fire in the grain fields. At approximately 17 years of age, Selma married. She had two boys and a girl in six years before being abandoned by her husband under circumstances similar to what is written here. Exactly how she survived that first winter of abandonment is not known. After that winter she survived by working for the Otto Wollerman family of Edgeley, ND. Their first meeting is also lost in time.

Otto Wollerman was an immigrant from West Prussia; prior to his immigration he had been a horse-trainer for the Kaiser's armies. His first wife died of tuberculosis in July of 1918. The following April, Selma and Otto married.

The years of Otto and Selma's acquaintance and marriage correspond roughly to World Wars I and II and the Great Depression. The early part of that era was still promising for late-immigrant farmers as grain prices held, lease-land was still plentiful, mechanization was flourishing, and the American agricultural infrastructure was modernizing. The middle part saw widespread failure and despair. When conditions began to change again in favor of the farmers, Otto and Selma's time had passed.

That is because in 1933 Otto Wollerman, by any evidence known, after a night of drinking, did shoot a man who had insulted Selma. Selma did not hear the insult first-hand. The transcript of Otto's court proceedings has been edited for length, and some names have been changed, but otherwise it is followed verbatim. Two of his letters from prison are also used verbatim.

Otto was apparently a model prisoner, since he was allowed to work in the fields as a trustee. In 1941 he was released, possibly due to ill health, and shortly thereafter he died of a stroke. During those few months of freedom, he began to re-establish his reputation as a good father and citizen.

During and after his imprisonment, Otto's family, in the barest of conditions, survived and grew mainly because of Selma's strength, perseverance, and domestic skills. Understandably, Selma and the children gradually quit speaking of Otto. When remembered it was for his weaknesses more than for his record as an honest and progressive farmer, a loving husband and father.

In 1944 Selma and Otto's son Fritz was killed in action in the South Pacific. The Wollerman children were treated badly by some neighbors after their father was imprisoned. Had their father been successful, all would likely have been well-educated at his insistence. Instead, family economics meant that most were on their own by age 14 or 15. Yet all became productive and durable citizens.

In the early 1980s, Selma did attend a family reunion at Bigfork, Montana, did proudly state that she had started all of this, did enjoy driving to the mountaintop, did wisecrack about the steep roads. However, she did not then or ever talk about her own or Otto's troubles at any length.

Alert and only recently confined to a wheelchair, Selma died in 1990 at 101 years of age, having outlived two husbands and two of her children. One of her granddaughters is Karen Jane Knickerbocker Rude, my wife since 1967.

It might well be asked: why attempt to resurrect these two people? And, since a detailed chronology of these lives is not recorded, can any re-telling be authentic? And, if their story is told in fiction, is that honest? And even if it can be told honestly, will dredging up the past be more harmful than valuable?

I can only answer this.

On a wall in my home is a large photo of Otto Wollerman looking every inch a skilled, arrogant Prussian cavalryman. I have been a bit haunted by that photo, wondering how a man so visibly certain of his position and capabilities, fell to imprisonment for a sordid murder, thus ruining his own life and making so difficult the life of his family.

In looking at the few artifacts of that proud man's life, and in listening to his children gradually, finally, begin in the 1990s to tell their children about him, I became convinced his story needed telling, though no one alive today can tell it in exact terms. I am not certain he could have done so himself.

But listening to what is left of his story also convinced me that Selma, "Grandma Wollerman" as I knew her briefly, was not the stereotype of the intellectually-deprived, all-suffering, submissive late-pioneer farm-wife, which, I admit, I thought she had been.

In fact, her life was most remarkable, filled with relentless privation and tragedy, yet she lived it all with skill, compassion, humility, humor, plain old toughness; she never asked for sympathy, never claimed the victim role, which spouts so easily from others with far fewer difficulties. She was a "strong woman" long before those words became popular, perhaps in a more profound way than the words are popularly used. And her attributes passed on powerfully to the next generations.

Thus, Otto's life held the elements of a classic tragedy, not only in his actions, but in how he was perceived by others. He was a dominant personality destroyed by a combination of circumstance and his own flaws. But when I viewed Selma's life beside Otto's, hers became a triumph.

It seemed to me then, that even if some old wounds are re-opened in the telling, these two lives were meant to be remembered.

I hope I have done them justice.

Ron Rude,
winter 2004

Printed in the United States
29444LVS00004B/202